John Skelton, John Ashton

A ballade of the Scottysshe kynge

John Skelton, John Ashton

A ballade of the Scottysshe kynge

ISBN/EAN: 9783744643306

Printed in Europe, USA, Canada, Australia, Japan

Cover: Foto ©Andreas Hilbeck / pixelio.de

More available books at **www.hansebooks.com**

The Earlieſt known Printed Engliſh Ballad.

A

BALLADE

OF THE

SCOTTYSSHE KYNGE.

WRITTEN BY

JOHN SKELTON,

POET LAUREATE TO KING HENRY THE EIGHTH.

REPRODUCED IN FACSIMILE WITH AN HISTORICAL

AND BIBLIOGRAPHICAL INTRODUCTION

BY

JOHN ASHTON.

LONDON:

ELLIOT STOCK, 62, PATERNOSTER ROW, E.C.

1882.

CONTENTS.

A BALLADE OF THE SCOTTYSSHE KYNGE.

CHAPTER I.

ORIGIN OF BALLADS.

F all varieties of poetry, the BALLAD, in the form which it affects among us, in diſtinction to other countries, is, perhaps, one of the moſt attractive. Although deriving its appellation from a word ſignifying a *dance* in Italy and France, where the ballad was a metrical narrative, or domeſtic epic, generally ſhort, or at leaſt not very long, as to its amount, and uſed as an accompaniment to a dance, the Engliſh ballad by no means demanded the dance for its accompaniment, and only ſignified a fairly ſhort narrative poem in a rhyming metre of a lively, tripping, and popular ſtyle, which could be ſung or chanted, and as ſuch, was eaſily diſtinguiſhed from the true

poem or lay, which was compofed in an artificial and
more ferious verfe, and was only intended for recita-
tion.   It is difficult, if not altogether impoffible, to
trace the origin of the prefent form of the ballad in
England.   There is great probability that it is contemporary with the times when the alliterative, or
initial-rhyming poems of the Anglo-Saxon and Early
Englifh poets were gradually giving way to the end-
rhyming poetry which Chaucer and his·school did fo
much to dignify.

Of our indigenous ballads, many fo-called collec-
tions have been compiled.   A mere lift of the titles
would be tedious and of little profit here.   Perhaps
the oldeft known example is that of " King Horn,"
derived from an older and unfound ballad, yet certainly written in the form in which it is now extant,
as early as the thirteenth century.   Another celebrated
and early ballad, "Gamelyn," is of the fourteenth
century.   After this period the ballad, in the elaftic
forms to which it lends itfelf both as to intrinfic narra-
tional character, and extrinfic metrical adaptation, provided only the quality of being capable of being fung
be preferved, fprings rapidly into vogue among the
copyifts, and examples of it abound.   In fact, for a
feafon, the ballad occupied a dignified pofition among
lefs facile forms of poetry.   It was a form favoured
by the beft poets, and admired by the moft apprecia-
tive lifteners.   But, after a time, as the progrefs of

education and the advance of literary tafte directed
the attention of the better claffes to other channels
of compofition, fo the ballad came to be neglected and
defpifed, until at length, particularly in the feventeenth
century, it degenerated into a vehicle for ribaldry,
obfcenity, and fcurrility, printed in the fimpleft and
commoneft manner, carried about the country by
pedlars who pandered to the depraved taftes of their
unlettered cuftomers, and, with few exceptions, worth-
lefs in every point of its former excellence. Curioufly
enough an exception muft be made with regard to the
Scottifh ballads, many of which, particularly thofe
relating to martial deeds, or military prowefs, are of
a far fuperior character to thofe of England, which are
found contemporary with them. The fimpler, chafter,
and more martial fpirit of the Caledonians, no doubt con-
tributed to this refult, and in turn was influenced by it.

Whether the curious " Ballade," which is the fubject of the prefent treatife, fhould take rank as the
earlieft known printed ballad in England—or only be
entitled to fecondary honours—mainly depends on
what can be termed a ballad—where a fong ends, and
a poem commences. It has, however, but one rival,
" The Nut-browne Mayd," to which the title of a ballad
can be hardly affigned in the fame fenfe of perfectnefs,
and felf-completenefs that this is.[1] This poem may

---

[1] It fhould be borne in mind that Mr. G. Barnett Smith com-

be familiar to many readers, but few know its pedigree, and title to rank as the earlieſt known printed ballad.

Early in the ſixteenth century a book was publiſhed at Antwerp, without date or author's name, and this, for want of a better name, has been called " Arnold's Chronicle," or " The Cuſtomes of London." Bale, Pits, Stowe, and Holinſhed, aſcribe this work to Arnold (according to Stowe, "a citizen of London "), "who being inflamed with the fervente love of good learninge, travailed very ſtudiouſly therin, and princi-

municated the text of this ballad to the "Athenæum," No. 2790, April 16, 1881, p. 525, with deſcriptive notes relating to the principal events in the progreſs of its diſcovery. This was followed in the next number, p. 561, by a paragraph containing an extract from a letter by Profeſſor Skeat to the editor, in which he writes: "I do not quite know why it is called the 'oldeſt Engliſh printed ballad.' The ballad of 'The Nut-brown Maid,' printed at length in my 'Specimens of Engliſh Literature,' is quite a famous one ; every one ſhould know of it who cares for Engliſh Literature. And it was printed in 1502." The ſame paragraph points out that the accuracy of Mr. Barnett Smith's tranſcript is impugned. To this Mr. Smith, in the "Athenæum," No. 2792, April 30, pp. 592, 593, replied that his variations conſiſt "in nearly every inſtance in the ſubſtitution of capital letters where they ſeem to be required, and in the uniform ſpelling of a word or two where the original was defective." In this reply, alſo, Mr. Smith admits having for the moment forgotten the claims of "The Nut-brown Maid" for a date of 1502,and he adds, "But after all it is a ſecondary matter whether 'The Nut-brown Maid' preceded by a few years the ballad of 'The Scottiſh King,' or whether the latter was the earlier in the order of publication. The one paramount fact is that here—as is generally believed—is a per-

pally in obferving matters worthy to be remembred of the pofteritye; he noted the Charters, liberties, lawes, conftitucions and Cuftomes of the Citie of London. He lived in the year 1519." Whether he, or any one elfe wrote the book, does not much matter; it is a book entirely on mercantile fubjeĉts, with the remarkable exception of the unexpeĉted, and uncalled-for, interpolation of the anonymous poem which has received the name of the " Nut-brown Mayd." The page in " Arnold's Chronicle," which precedes this poem, confifts of " The compoficion betwene the marchauntis of england and yᵉ towne of

feĉtly new ballad, which muft poffefs a ftrong and genuine intereft for men of letters and antiquaries.'' Mr. Adin Williams, another correfpondent to the fame periodical, in the fame column, chal-lenges Profeffor Skeat's ftatement that the date of 1502 is to be affigned to "The Nut-brown Maid," and inclines to 1521 as a nearer date of publication, although the ballad was written about the earlier date mentioned. He fays in continuation, "Mr. Barnett Smith might call his the oldeft printed ballad, with title-page and date, iffued as a book, and not as a portion of a book, even if Arnold's 'Chronicle' is faid to have been printed before 1521. But what of the 'Gefte of Robin Hood,' Edinburgh, 1508?" Profeffor Skeat, however, in a fubfequent communication (No. 2793, May 7, p. 623) completely demolifhes this affertion by fhowing that there are two old editions of Arnold's "Chronicle," one printed in 1502, and the other in 1521, and fuggefts the date of the writing of " The Nut-brown Maid" as " about 1500, but that is the very lateft date that can be reafonably accepted." To this Mr. A. Williams acquiefces in the following No. 2974, May 14, p 654.

andwarp, for the coſtis of ther marchaundicis brought
to the ſaid towne and leauing thens." Immediately
before the poem is " Brokers to pay for a cloth under
xl.s. the broker ſhal haue ij.g7.

Item for a cloth aboue xl.s. the broker hath iiij.g7.
Item C. ellis cotton cloth payth lyke a clothe iiij.g7. &c"

and immediately after it the book continues the even,
buſineſs-like tenour of its way, and dilates upon " The
rekenyng to bey waris in flaundres." The date of
1502 or 1503 has been aſcribed to the " Chronicle ",
ſolely for the reaſon that the laſt ſheriffs in the com-
piler's liſt, in the firſt edition, are Henry Keble and
Nicolas Nynes, in the 18th year of King Henry
VIII., viz., 1502. This date may or may not be
rightly aſcribed, and need only be queſtioned if the
title of the poem of the " Nut-brown Maid " to be
conſidered a ballad ſtands good.

What is a ballad ? or rather what *was* a ballad ?
for we all know its preſent meaning. Chaucer and
others uſed the term " balade " for a ſong written in
a particular rhythm, but that definition paſſed away,
and it came certainly to mean a popular ſong on ſome
warlike feat, or adventure, love or intrigue, of more
or leſs extent, but ſtill ſhort enough to be ſung, and,
as I take it, to be ſung by one perſon only, there
being no antiphonal ballads properly ſo called. But
the whole of the " Nut-brown Maid " from the

twenty-fecond line (out of 180) is a metrical dialogue
between the knight and the maid, and is, moreover,
intended to be fo:—

Line 13. "Than betwene vs, lete vs difcuffe, what was all the
maner
14. Be twene them too, we wyl alfo, telle all they peyne
in fere
15. That fhe was in, *now I begynne, foo that ye me anfwere*."

This removes it at once out of the category of a *ballad*.
That it has hitherto been thus defcribed is of no im-
portance, and, until this " ballade of the Scottyfhe
Kynge " was found, it was fcarcely worth while to
remove the " Nut-brown Maid " from the poft of
honour. Profeffor Skeat and others have, neverthe-
lefs, accepted this as a ballad ; and granting that the
" Nut-brown Maid " thoroughly fulfils all the condi-
tions of a ballad, I ftill claim the higheft honours for
the " Scottyfshe Kynge," on the ground that it is inde-
pendently publifhed, that it has a title and a colophon,
and that it ftyles itfelf a ballad, thus leaving no doubt
as to its charaćter. It, therefore, ftands at prefent as
the earlieft printed Englifh ballad.

CHAPTER II.

DESCRIPTION OF THE BALLADE OF THE SCOTTYSSHE

KYNGE.

HE defcription of this poem in the Britifh Mufeum Catalogue is as follows :—

"James IV. King of Scotland. A ballade of the Scottyfshe Kynge (commencing 'Kynge Jamy, Jomy your Joye is all go;') on the battle of Floddon by John Skelton, B.L. Richard Fawkes. London, 1513. 4°. Note. 4 leaves without title page or pagination. 31 lines to the full page. Beneath the title is a woodcut reprefenting two Knights; and beneath the woodcut are the firft four lines of the letterprefs. This ballad was included in 'a treatyfe of the Scottes' publifhed later among 'Certayne bokes cōpyled by Mayfter Skelton' but with many variations. It is believed to be the firft printed Englifh Ballad."

As far as is known this piece is unique, and its

hiftory is fomewhat romantic. On opening the book is found the pen-and-ink note :—

"'A ballade of the Scottyfshe Kynge.' This formed the infide of the wooden cover of an old folio volume belonging to Mifs Chafyn Grove of Zeals Houfe, Bath. The old book, with a great many more, had lain for years on the floor of a garret in a farm houfe at Whaddon, co. Dorfet (now Mifs Grove's), and both farm houfe and library had come to her by family defcent, from Mr. Bullen Reynes of co. Dorfet.

> "J. E. Jackfon,
> "Leigh Delamere,
> "Chippenham,
> "Hon. Canon of Briftol.
> "Nov. 9, 1878."

This authentication is, however, fomewhat meagre, and it is a pity that Canon Jackfon did not enter more fully into the details of its difcovery. It was found, as defcribed, in the cover of the French romance of "Huon of Bordeaux," printed at Paris by Michel le Noir in 1513, which was bound in oak after its arrival in England. Not the leaft remarkable circumftance connected with its finding, was that in the other fide cover of the book, were two leaves of a very fcarce tract on Floddon Field, "The trewe encountre or . . Batayle lately don betwene Englade and: Scotlande. In whiche batayle the . Scottfshe

Kynge was ſlayne" and known to be printed by
Richard Faques.[1] This gave an opportunity of comparing the type and printing of the ballad and proſe
narrative, and proved that both were the work of
Faques, who, indeed, printed at leaſt one other book
of Skelton's.[2] In this I moſt fully concur, having had

[1] "Richard Fawkes, Faques, or Fakes, is thought by Bagford
in his MS. Memoranda, to have been a foreigner, and to have
printed in the Monaſtery of Syon, while one Myghel Fawkes
printed in conjunction with Robert Copland in 1535. There is
greater probability in the ſuppoſition that Fawkes was a relation
of William Faques the king's printer (who printed from 1499 to
1508). Few of his books exhibit the ſame ſkilfulneſs of execution
as do thoſe of this latter printer. 'However that be (adds Herbert), Mr Thomas Wilſon of Leeds in Yorkſhire, in a letter to
Mr. Ames, dated April 2, 1751, informed him that Richard
Fawkes, printer, was ſecond ſon of John Fawkes of Farnley Hall,
Eſqre, in the ſaid County ; and that in a pedigree he has, of that
family, he is called Printer of London.' There is a looſe MS.
note in Herbert's 'Memoranda Books' that Wyer was ſervant
to Fawkes ; but I have never diſcovered a volume in which ſuch
teſtimony appears. . . . . . Time has ſpared very few of his publi-
cations, and his books may be treaſured among the rarities of the
typographical art."—" Typographical Antiquities," &c., by the
Rev. Thomas Frognall Dibdin, vol. iii., p. 355, ed. 1816.

[2] "Skelton's Garlande or Chapelet of Laurell," 1523. Quarto.

" A ryght delectable tratyſe vpon a goodly Garlande or Chapelet of Laurell by mayſter Skelton Poete laureat ſtudyouſly dyuyſed
at Sheryfhotton Caſtell. In yᵉ foreſte of galtres/ wherein ar cō-
pryſyde many & dyuers ſolacyons & ryghte pregnant allectyves
of ſyngular pleaſure/ as more at large it doth apere in yᵉ pces
folowynge "

" ⁋ Inpryntyd by me Rycharde faukes dwellydg in durā rent

an opportunity of comparing them. It feems, however, that this fortunate difcovery was to be full of
furprifes, for thefe two leaves were the very ones
wanting to complete the copy of this tract in the
library of S. Chriftie Miller, Efq., of Craigentinny,
and Britwell, Bucks. The Ballad would, in all probability have remained ftill longer unknown to the
general public, as it was somewhat hidden; being
catalogued, as we have feen, under the· heading
"James IV. King of Scotland"—had it not been
kindly pointed out to me by Mr. Anderfon of the
Britifh Mufeum, who knew my fondnefs for ancient
ballad literature.

The ballad, although not dated, carries with it in-
ternal evidence of its date. Indeed, Skelton was in
fuch hafte to fing his pæan, that he evidently acted
on the firft (and incorrect) verfion of the victory.
It is probable that he did not know of the death of
King James; at any rate, he fpeaks of him all through
as living as a prifoner at Norham :—

> "For to the Caftell of Norham
> I vnderftonde to foone ye cam.
> For a pryfoner there now ye be
> Eyther to the devyll or the trinitie."

er els in Powlis chyrche yarde at the fygne of the 𝕬.𝕭.𝕮.
The yere of our lorde god. 𝕸.𝕮𝕮𝕮𝕮𝖗𝖗iij. The. iij. day of
Octobre."

And again :—

> " Of the Kynge of nauerne ye may take hede/
> How vnfortunately he doth now fpede/
> In double welles now he dooth dreme.
> That is a Kynge witou a realme
> At hym example ye wolde none take
> Experyence hath brought you in the fame brake."

When Skelton re-wrote the ballad, and publifhed it years after, in " Skelton Laureate againft the Scottes," he was aware of this anachronifm and altered it :—

> " Unto the caftell of Norram
> I vnderftande, to fone ye came
> Thus for your guerdon quyt ar ye
> Thanked be God in Trinitie."

> " Of the Kyng of Nauerne, ye might take heed
> Ungracioufly how he doth fpeed
> In double delynge, fo he did dreme
> That he is Kynge, without a Reme.
> And for example he would none take
> Experiens hath brought you in fuch a brake."

Skelton evidently confidered it important to be early in the field, and as, from his pofition as poet laureate and the King's orator, he muft needs be loyal above all to his royal mafter, and thoroughly fevere upon his enemies, he called upon Melpomene—

> " To guyde my pen, and my pen to embibe
> Illumine me your poet and your fcribe

That with mixture of Aloes and bitter gall
I may compound, confectures for accordiall
To angre the Scottes, and Irifk Kiteringes withal
That late were difcomfect, with battaile marcial."

If he could do this, and fing his fong of triumph,
there was no need of delay until authentic news of the
victory arrived,—fo he fet himfelf to do as he fays :—

"So that now I haue deuifed
And in my minde I haue comprifed
Of the proude Scot, King Jemmy
To write fome lytell tragedy
For no manner confideration
Of any forowful lamentation
But for our fpecial confolacion
Of al our royal Englyfh Nacion."

CHAPTER III.

BIOGRAPHICAL NOTICES OF JOHN SKELTON.

AVING thus eſtabliſhed the authorſhip, of the ballad, it will be advantageous to put on record ſome notices of Skelton himſelf. There are ſeveral quaſi portraits of Skelton extant—but there is only one likely to be at all reliable. In the " Chapelet of Laurell " is one, but that is evidently from the ſame block that repreſents the month of April in " le cōpoſt et kalendrier des bergeres " printed by Guy Marchāt, Paris, 1499. There was another portrait in an edition of " Dyuers Balletys and Dyties ſolacious "; but as this alſo did duty for Dr. Boorde (author of Wiſe Men of Gotham, &c.), it cannot be received as genuine. It ſeems ſingular, that, ſeeing he was a well-known character, and popular writer, old woodcuts ſhould have to do duty for his " vera effigies " ; but ſuch is the caſe.

Another portrait in an edition of " Colin Clout "

printed by Richard Kele, is, to fay the leaft, very dubious, judging by previous experience ; but there is one,—in "Portraits Illuftrating Granger's Biographical Hiftory of England," commonly known as Richardfon's Colle&ion, which really does feem a probable likenefs— a flat black cap forms the headpiece of a frank fmiling face, which is rather broad, and with pointed chin. He wears a flight beard and mouftache. He is dreffed in a black caffock and coat, with a collar flightly laced, hair rather fhort and curling, ears fomewhat prominent.

The only attempt at authenticating this portrait is, that it is " from an original picture in the poffeffion of Mr. Richardfon."

His birthplace is unknown, fome imagining he was born in Norfolk, others that he came from Cumberland, and we are in equal ignorance as to the date of his birth. It is affumed that it could not be earlier than 1460, and the reafoning by which this furmife has been arrived at, is that probably one of the earlieft poems he wrote was that " Of the Death of the Noble prince Kynge Edwarde the forth ", who died 1483. It is certain that he ftudied at Oxford, and was laureated there fomewhere about 1490, for in the preface to " the boke of Eneydos compyled by Vyrgyle," which was tranflated from the French by Caxton, and publifhed by him in 1490, we find " But I praye mayfter John Skelton, late created poete laureate in the vnyuerfite of oxenford, to ouerfee and correct this fayd booke." Search was made in the Oxford records by the Rev. Dr. Blifs, who was unable to find any trace of Skelton's diftinction, but the poet himfelf fays :—

> " At Oxforth the vniverfyte
> Auaunfid I was to that degre ;
> By hole confent of theyr fenate,
> I was made poete laureat."[1]

Shortly after, the Univerfity of Cambridge conferred an *ad eundem* degree on him. " An. Dom. 1493 et Hen. 7. nono. Conceditur Johi Skelton Poete in partibus tranfmarinis[2] atque Oxon. Laurea ornato, ut apud nos eadem decoraretur," and in 1504-5 this was again mentioned, and the right of wearing the habit which the King had granted was conceded to him. He was not a little proud of this habit, and in his poems againft Garnefche he mentions it feveral times.

> " What eylythe thé, rebawde, on me to raue ?
> A Kyng to me myn habyte gaue : "

It feems to have been white and green, and exceedingly fine, for he fays :—

> " Your fworde ye fwere, I wene,
> So tranchaunt and fo kene,
> Xall Kyl both wyght and grene :
> Your foly is to grett
> The Kynges colours to threte."

---

[1] " Skelton Laureate defendar ageinft lufty Garnyfhe well befeen Chryftofer Chalangar, et cetera " lines 81-4.

[2] Louvain, where he had alfo ftudied.

On this habit, or on fome other portion of his attire, the name of his Mufe Calliope was embroidered.

"Why were ye *Calliope* embrawdred with letters of golde ?
Skelton Laureate. Orato. Reg. maketh this aunfwere &c—
Calliope
As ye may fe,
Regent is fhe
Of poetes al,
Whiche gaue to me
The high degre
Laureat to be
Of fame royall ;
Whofe name enrolde
With filke and golde
I dare be bolde
Thus for to were
Of her I holde
And her houfholde ;
Though I waxe olde
And fomedele ferc
Yet is fhe fayne,
Voyde of difdayn,
Me to retayne
Her feruiture :
With her certayne
I will remayne
As my fouerayne
Mooft of pleafure
Maulgre touz malheureux."

Skelton followed the cuftom of moft learned men of that age, he entered the Church, and was admitted to the grade of fubdeacon on the 31ft March, deacon

c

14th April, and ordained prieſt 9th June, A.D. 1498.
It is uncertain when he was appointed tutor to Prince
Henry, afterwards Henry VIII., but he had baſked
in the ſunſhine of court favour for ſome time pre-
viouſly, for he celebrated the creation of Prince
Arthur as Prince of Wales and Earl of Cheſter in
A.D. 1489 in a compoſition called " Prince Arthur's
Creacyoun,"—a piece which is not now extant,—and
when Prince Henry was created Duke of York in
A.D. 1494, Skelton ſeized the opportunity of dedica-
ting ſome Latin verſes to his patron.   He ſeems alſo
to have attended to the ſtudies of his young charge,
for he writes,[1]

> "The Duke of Yorkis creauncer whan Skelton was
> Now Henry the VIII. Kyng of Englonde,
> A Tratyſe he deuyſid and browght it to pas,
> Callid *Speculum Principis*, to bere in his honde
> Therin to rede ; and to vnderſtande
> All the demenour of princely aſtate,
> To be our Kyng, of God preordinate."

No date has been aſſigned to his appointment as
Rector of Difs in Norfolk, which preferment he ſeems
to have held till his death, but that he had the living
in 1504 there can be no doubt, for his ſignature
" Maſter John Skelton. Laureat. Parſon of Diſſe,"
appears as a witneſs to the will of Mary Cooper of
Difs in that year.   Here, however, he came under

---

[1] " Garlande of Laurell."

the heavy difpleafure of his diocefan, Nix or Nykke, on account of his marriage, conduct which would hardly call forth fuch a heavy punifhment now-a-days.[1]

[1] In 1873 Mr. Walter de Gray Birch, F.S.A., difcovered among the MSS. of Mr. William Bragge, F.S.A., at Sheffield, an unpublifhed lyric by Skelton referring to this epifode in the domeftic life of the poet. From the allufion to the feparation of a hufband and wife, when the latter was "ny off progeny," we may fairly conclude that it was written fhortly after Skelton's enforced feparation from his wife, during his refuge at Weftminfter. The poem, which formed the fubject of a communication by Mr. Birch to the "Athenæum," is as follows:—

" Petevelly
Conftraynd am y   } to morne and playne.
With weepyng y

" Thatt we fo ny
off progeny   } Schuld parte on twayne.
So fodenly

" When yee are goyn
Conforte ys noyne   } Endewre muft y.
Butt al a looyne

" With grevyly groyne
Makyng my moyne   } That fchuld nedys dy.
As hytt where oone

" With chance fodyne
Soo doythe me ftrayne } That for no thyng,
Yn every wayne

" I cannott layne
Nor yeet refrayne   } Frome foore wepyng."
Myne yes tweyne

Fuller[1] fays "The Dominican Friars were the next
he contefted with, whofe vitioufnefs lay pat enough
for his hand; but fuch foul Lubbers fell heavy on all
which found fault with them. Thefe inftigated Nix
Bifhop of Norwich, to call him to account for keeping
a Concubine, which coft him, (as it feems) a fufpenfion
from his benefice. . . . . . We muft not forget
how being charged by fome on his death bed for be-
getting many children on the aforefaid Concubine; he
protefted, that in his Confcience he kept her in the
notion of a wife, though fuch his cowardlinefs that he
would rather confefs adultery, (then accounted but a
venial;) than own Marriage efteemed a capital crime
in that age."

But one can hardly fancy jovial, hard-hitting
Skelton, whofe "talke was as he wraet," as a prieft.
As Anthony Wood[2] fays of him, he "was efteemed
more fit for the ftage than the pew or pulpit," and,
indeed, the "certayne merye tales of Skelton, Poet
Lauriat," countenance the affertion; and the old ftory
of "Long Meg of Weftminfter" fhows him as drink-
ing at an inn with his hoftefs, a Spanifh knight called
Sir James of Caftille, and Will Somers, and fpeaks of
him as being in "his mad merrie vein." Churchyarde writes that he was "feldom out of Princis grace"

---

[1] "The Hiftory of the Worthies of England endeavoured by
Thomas Fuller, D.D." Lond. 1662, p. 257.
[2] Blifs' edition of "Ath. Oxon.," vol. i., p. 50.

—he had the favour both of his royal mafter and of
Cardinal Wolfey.   He was clofely allied in friendfhip
with the latter in 1519, for " Lautre envoy " to the
"Garlande of Laurell " is dedicated "Ad fereniffimam
maieftatem regiam, pariter cum domino Cardinali
Legato a latere honorificatiffimo, &c.," and Wolfey
was not fole legate until that year, having previoufly
been joined with Campeggio.   Another paffage in his
works fhows he enjoyed the cardinal's favour.   We
read in "Lenvoy" appended to " Howe the douty
duke of Albany, lyke a cowarde knyght, ran awaye
fhamfully with an hundred thoufande tratlande fcottes
and faint harted frenchemen: befide the water of
Twede, &c." :—

> "Skelton Laureat. obfequious et loyall
> To my lorde Cardynals right noble grace, &c.
>
> Lenvoy.
>
> Go lytell quayre apace
> In mooft humble wyfe
> Before his noble grace
> That caufed you to deuife
> This lytel enterprife
> And hym mooft lowly pray
> In hys mynde to comprife
> Thofe wordes his grace dyd faye
> Of an ammas gray.
>   Je, Foy enterment
>   En fa bone grace."

On account of a circumftance, the reafon of which

has not yet been made apparent, his pen fo lafhed the
cardinal, efpecially in " Why come ye not to Court,"
which is a grofs perfonal attack, and " Speake parrot,"
that his eminence became his better enemy.   And
this is not to be wondered at, for in the former poem
Skelton rails violently againft him.   We may take
one or two paffages out of feveral, for example :—

"But this mad Amalecke.
Like to Amamalek
He regardeth Lordes
No more than potfhordes
He is in fuch elacion
Of his exaltacion
And the fupportacion
Of our Soueraine Lorde
He ruleth al at will
Without reafon or fkyll
Howbeit they be prymordyall
Of hys wretched originall
And his bafe progeny
And his grefy genealogy
He came of the ranke roiall
That was caft out of a bouchers ftall

*   *   *   *

For he was parde
No doctour of devinitie
Nor doctor of the law.
Nor of none other faw.
But a poore maifter of arte

*   *   *   *

God faue hys noble grace
And graunt him a place
Endleffe to dwel
With the deuill of hel
For and he were there
We nead neuer feare
Of the feendes blacke
For I vndertake
He wold fo brag and Crake
That he wold than make
The deuils to quake."

The cardinal caufed meafures to be taken with a view to apprehend him, but Skelton fled, and took fanctuary at Weftminfter with his old friend Abbot Iflip. There he remained moft probably until his death, which occurred 21ft June, 1529. He was buried in the chancel of St. Margaret's, Weftminfter.

The quaint poet Churchyarde thus writes of the departed Laureate :—

" Ohe fhall I leaue out Skeltons name
    The bloffome of my frute
The tree wheron indeed
    My branchis all might groe
Nay Skelton wore the Laurell wreath
    And paft in Schoels ye knoe.
A poet for his arte,
    Whoes iudgment fuer was hie,
And had great practies of the pen,
    His works they will not lie.
His terms to taunts did lean,
    His talk was as he wraet :

Full quick of witte, right ſharp of words,
    And ſkilfull of the ſtaet.
Of reaſon riep and good,
    And to the haetfull mynd :
That did diſdain his doings ſtill,
    A ſkornar of his kynd.
Moſt pleaſant euery way,
    As poets ought to be :
And ſeldom out of Princis grace
    And great with eche degre."

It has been the faſhion to criticiſe Skelton for the language which he uſed.   Pope even went ſo far as to call him " beaſtly Skelton," and Miſs Agnes Strickland was particularly ſevere upon him ; but theſe writers ignore the ſtate of ſociety as it then was, and forget that both Rabelais and Skelton wrote for a purpoſe ; Southey with better diſcernment ſays : " Unleſs Skelton had written thus for the coarſeſt palates he could not have poured forth his bitter and undaunted ſatire in ſuch perilous times."

CHAPTER IV.

THE BATTLE OF FLODDON.

HE battle of Floddon has had many chroniclers, and ftudents of hiftory are familiar with its details, but it is neceffary, in order thoroughly to underftand Skelton's ballad, that the ground fhould be gone over yet once again.

James IV., King of Scots, was in the feventeenth year of his age when he afcended the throne, having been born 17 May, 1471, and yet even at this early age he had paffed through much trouble. He never ceafed to bear in mind that his father's fad and violent death had placed him upon the throne; reached as it was by the fearful ftep of filial rebellion. The confederate barons rofe againft James III., who marched on Stirling, where Shaw, the governor of the caftle and guardian to the young prince, refufed him admiffion. The confederates approached, and the prince joined them,

ſo that both ſides diſplayed the Royal Standard. It
was at Sauchie Burn, between Bannockburn and
Stirling, that the armies joined. The fight was very far
from deſperate, but the timorous king fled. His grey
horſe galloping along, was frightened by a miller's wife
dropping the pitcher which ſhe was filling at a well,
and the king was thrown to the ground. He was
carried into the miller's houſe and laid on a bed, where
he diſcloſed himſelf, and deſired that a prieſt ſhould be
ſummoned to ſhrive him. The woman ran out calling
for a prieſt for the king, and a man who was paſſing
at the time, under pretence of performing this laſt
office of the church, entered the houſe and ſtooped
over the king's bed, and ſtabbed him many times. The
feigned prieſt fled, and was never found.[1]

---

[1] Lindſay's "Chronicles of Scotland" gives the following account of the king's death:—" Cuming throw the toun of Bannockburne, ane voman perceaved ane man cuming faſt vpoun hors, ſhoe
being carrieing in watter, cam faſt away and left the jug behind
her ; ſo the Kingis hors lap the burne and ſlak of friewill quhair-
fra the voman cam. The King being evill ſittin, (*i.e.* riding badly)
fell aff his hors befoir the mylne doore of Bannockburne, and ſo
was bruiſed with the fall, being heavie in armour, that he fell in
ane deadlie ſowne : And the miller and his wayff harled him into
the mylne, and not knowing quhat he was, keſt him vp in ane nuik
and covered him with ane cloath ; . . . . And be the Kingis
enemies war reteiring back, the King himſelff over came lying
in the mylne, and cryed, if thair was ane preiſt to mak his
confeſſioun. The myller and his wayff heiring thir wordis, in-
quyred of him quhat man he was, and what was his name. He

His father's death preyed upon young James's mind, for although he was not actively affociated with it, yet he could not but deem himfelf to have been in fome refpects the caufe of the king's tragic end, as he was in arms againft his father at the time.

Holinfhed fays : " his eldeft fon James the fourth was crowned King of Scotland and began his reigne the 24 of June in the yeare 1488 being not paft fixteene yeeres of age, who notwithftanding that he had beene in the field with the nobles of the realme againft his father, that contrarie to his mind was flaine ; yet neuertheleffe afterwards, hee became a right noble prince & feemed to take great repentance for that his offenfe, and in token therof, he ware continuallie an iron chaine about his midle all the daies of his life."

happened to fay, vnhappilie ' This day at morne I was your King' Than the milleris wayff clapped her handis, and ran furth and cryed for ane prieft. In this meane tyme ane prieft was cuming by ; fum fays he was my lord Grayes fervand ; quho anfweired and faid " heir am I ane preift, quhair is the King ? " Then the milleris wayff tuik the prieft by the hand, and led him in at the mylne doore, and how foone the faid preift faw the King, he knew him incontinent, and kneilled doun on his knies, and fpeired at the Kingis grace if he might live if he had guid leichment : he anfweired him he trowed he might bot he wold have had a preift to tak his adwyce, and to give him his facrament. The preift anfweired, that fall I doe haiftilie,—and pulled out ane whinger, and ftrak him four or fyve tymes evin to the heart, and fyne gatt him on his back and had him away. Bot no man knew quhat he did with him, nor quhair he buried him."

This chain he increafed in weight every year by the addition of another link, and it was the abfence of this chain on the king's body when found after the battle of Floddon that caufed the rumour that he was not killed, but had efcaped, and would come again to reign over his country.

CHAPTER V.

THER principal events connected with England in the reign of James IV. are the affiftance and countenance which the king gave to Perkin Warbeck, and his marriage with Margaret, the daughter of Henry VII., with whom he received a portion of £10,000, a jointure of £2,000 per annum, and yearly pin money to the value of £331 6s. 8d. being fettled by the king on his confort. The royal pair were married in June, 1502, Margaret being taken to her hufband by the very Earl of Surrey who was deftined afterwards to meet the king, and conquer him at Floddon. The old chronicler[1] tells the ftory very quaintly, "On the fixteenth of June King Henrie tooke his iournie from Richmond, with his daughter the faid ladie Margaret, and came to

[1] Holinfhed.

Coliwefton, where his mother the Counteffe of Richmond then laie. And after he had remained there certeine daies in paftime and great folace, he tooke leaue of his daughter, giuing her his bleffing with a fatherly exhortation, and committed the conveiance of hir into Scotland vnto the earle of Surreie, and others. The earle of Northumberland, as then warden of the marches, was appointed to deliuer hir vpon the borders vnto the king of Scotland. And fo this faire ladie was conveied with a great companie of lords, ladies, knights, efquires, and gentlemen, untill fhe came to the towne of Berwike, and from thence vnto Lambert church in Lamermoore within Scotland, where fhe was receiued by the king and all the nobles of that realme, and from the faid place of Lamberton church, fhe was conveied vnto Edenburgh, where the day after hir comming thither, fhe was maried vnto the faid king with great and folemne triumph to the high reioifing of all that were prefent."

But, as hiftory not infrequently fhows, marriage between fcions of royal houfes does not neceffarily produce clofe and continued amity between the nations, and the caufes which led to the difaftrous battle of Floddon were not likely to be overcome by fuch relationfhip. Of all hiftorians whofe refearches have led them to treat of this fubject, Lingard gives the terfeft and cleareft account of the various events which

led James to war with England. The paffage is
worthy to be quoted in its entirety. Of the marriage
between James and Margaret, the hiftorian writes,
" This new connection did not, however, extinguifh
the hereditary partiality of the Scottifh prince for the
ancient alliance with France ; and his jealoufy of his
Englifh brother was repeatedly irritated by a fucceffion
of real or fuppofed injuries. 1. James had frequently
claimed, but claimed in vain, from the equity of
Henry, the valuable jewels which the late king had
bequeathed as a legacy to his daughter, the Scottifh
queen. 2. In the laft reign he had complained of
the murder of Sir Robert Ker, the warden of the
Scottifh marches, and had pointed out the baftard
Heron of Ford as the affaffin ; and yet neither Heron,
nor his chief accomplices, had been brought to trial.
3. Laftly, he demanded juftice for the death of Andrew
Barton. As long ago as 1476, a fhip belonging to
John Barton had been plundered by a Portuguefe
fquadron ; and in 1506, juft thirty years afterwards,
James granted to Andrew, Robert and John, the
three fons of Barton, letters of reprifal, authorizing
them to capture the goods of Portuguefe merchants,
till they fhould have indemnified themfelves to the
amount of twelve thoufand ducats. But the adven-
turers found their new profeffion too lucrative to be
quickly abandoned ; they continued to make feizures
for feveral years ; nor did they confine themfelves to

veffels failing under the Portuguefe flag, but captured
Englifh merchantmen, on the pretence that they
carried Portuguefe property. Wearied out by the
clamour of the fufferers, Henry pronounced the Bar-
tons pirates, and the lord Thomas and Sir Edward
Howard, with the king's permiffion, boarded and captured two of their veffels in the Downs. In the action
Andrew Barton received a wound, which proved
fatal; the furvivors were fent by land into Scotland.
James confidered the lofs of Barton, the braveft and
moft experienced of his naval commanders, as a
national calamity; he declared it a breach of the peace
between the two crowns; and in the moft peremptory
tone demanded full and immediate fatisfaction. Henry
fcornfully replied, that the fate of a pirate was un-
worthy the notice of kings, and that the difpute,
if the matter admitted of difpute, might be fettled by
the Commiffioners of both nations at their next meeting
on the borders.

" While James was brooding over thefe caufes of
difcontent, Henry had joined in the league againft
Louis; and from that moment the Scottifh court
became the fcene of the moft active negotiations, the
French Ambaffadors claiming the aid of Scotland, the
Englifh infifting on its neutrality. The former ap-
pealed to the poverty and the chivalry of the king.
Louis made him repeated and valuable prefents of
money; Anne, the French queen, named him her

knight, and fent him a ring from her own finger.
He cheerfully renewed the ancient alliance between
Scotland and France, with an additional claufe recipro-
cally binding each prince to help his ally againft all
men whomfoever. Henry could not be ignorant that
this provifion was aimed againft himfelf; but he had
no reafon to complain; for in the laft treaty of peace,
the kings of England and Scotland had referved to
themfelves the power of fending military aid to any of
their friends, provided that aid were confined to de-
fenfive operations.

"It now became the objeét of the Englifh envoys
to bind James to the obfervance of peace during the
abfence of Henry. Much diplomatic fineffe was dif-
played by each party. To every projeét prefented by
the Englifh the Scottifh cabinet affented, but with
this perplexing provifo, that in the interval no incur-
fion fhould be made beyond the French frontier. Each
negotiated and armed at the fame time. It had been
agreed that, to redrefs all grievance, an extraordinary
meeting of commiffioners fhould be held on the borders
during the month of June. Though in this arrange-
ment both parties aéted with equal infincerity, the
Englifh gave the advantage to their opponents, by
demanding an adjournment to the middle of Oétober.
Their objeét could not be concealed. Henry was
already in France; and James having fummoned his
fubjeéts to meet him on Burrow Moor, defpatched his

D

fleet with a body of three thoufand men to the affis-
tance of Louis."

This very clear and concife hiftorical account brings
us down to the time of the ballad, which I fhall en-
deavour, as far as poffible, to illuftrate by extracts from
the writings of contemporary, or nearly contemporary,
hiftorians.

CHAPTER VI.

CONTEMPORARY EVIDENCE RELATING TO THE BALLAD.

 ORD HERBERT was then befieging Tereouenne, a town in the province of Artois, to the fouth-eaft of Calais, and the Earl of Shrewfbury had been fent with a divifion to fupport him, when on 21 July, 1513, Henry marched out of Calais, with an army of 15,000 horfe and foot. Near Ardres they encountered a ftrong detachment of French cavalry, who however withdrew, having executed a part of their miffion, that of fupplying the town with provifions and ammunition. He joined the forces of Lord Herbert and the Earl of Shrewfbury, and fat down before the town, whofe fiege was to be fo flow, and whofe ultimate fate was deftruction. However, unpropitious weather prevented the Englifh king from occupying the wonderful pavilion of filk and cloth of gold and blue damafk, and he had to inhabit a wooden houfe. The fiege progreffed until, to ufe the words of the chronicler

from whom I fhall have occafion prefently to quote
confiderably [1]:—·" The xi daie of Auguft beying thurf-
day, the Kynge lyeing at the fiege of Tyrwyn, had
knowlege that Maximilian thēperour was in yᵉ towne
of Ayre.   The Kyng prepared al thinges neceffarie
to mete with themperour in triumph.   The noble
men of the Kynges camp were gorgeoufly apparelled,
ther courfers barded with cloth of gold, of damafke &
broderie, there apparell all tiffue cloth of gold and
fyluer, and gold fmithes woorke, great cheynes of
balderickes of gold and belles of bullion, but in
efpecial yᵉ duke of Buckingham, he was in purple
fatten, his apparel and his barde full of Antelopes and
fwannes of fyne gold bullion and full of fpangyls and
littell belles of gold meruelous coftly and pleafãt to
behold.   The Kyng was in a garment of greate riches
in iuels as perles and ftone, he was armed in a light
armure, the mafter of hys horfe folowed him with a
fpare horfe, the henxmen folowed beryng the Kyngs
peces of harnys, euery one mounted on a greate courfer,
the one bare the helme, the feconde his graūgarde, the
thirde his fpere, the fourth his axe, and fo euery one
had fome thyng belonging to a man of armes ; the
apparell of the ix henxmen were white clothe of
golde and crymfyn cloth of gold, richely embrawdered
with goldefmythes woorke, the trappers of the corfets
were mantell harneys coulpened, and in every vent a

---

[1] Hall, edit. 1548.

longe bel of fyne gold, and on euery pendant a depe
taffel of fyne gold in bullion, whiche trappers were
very ryche. The Kyng and themperour met between
ayre and the camp, in the fowleft wether that lightly
hath bene fene. Themperour gentely enterteined the
Kyng, and the Kyng lykewyfe hym, and after a littell
communicacion had betwene them by caufe the wether
was foule, departed for that tyme. The Emperor and
all his men were at that daie all in black Cloth for the
Emprice his wife was lately diffeafed." Maximilian
had come nominally to place himfelf as a volunteer
under Henry.

We now come to that portion of the eventful time
which more particularly belongs to our fubject :—
" After that the Kyng was thus retorned to his campe,
within a day or twayne ther arryued in the army a
Kyng of Armes of Scotläd called Lyon with his cote
of armes on his back, and defyred to fpeke with the
Kyng, who within fhorte tyme was by Garter cheffe
Kynge of armes brought to the Kinges prefence,
where he beying almoft difmayed feynge the Kyng fo
nobly accompanied, with few woordes and metely
good reuerence, deliuered a letter to the King, which
receued yᵉ letter and redde it him felfe, and when he
had redde it, without any more delay, he hym felfe
aunfwered after this forte. Nowe we perceyue the
Kynge of Scottes our brother in law & your mafter
to be yᵉ fame perfon whom we euer toke hym to be,

for we neuer eſtemed hym to be of any truthe & ſo
nowe we haue founde it, for notwithſtandynge his
othe, his promiſe in yᵉ woorde of Kynge & his owne
hand and ſeale, yet now he hath brokẽ his faithe and
promiſe to his great diſhonour and infamie for euer,
and entendeth to inuade our realme in our abſence
whiche he dirſt not ones attempte, our perſon beynge
preſente, but he ſheweth himſelfe not to be degenerate
from the condicions of his forefathers, whoſe faythes
for the moſt parte hath euer byn violated and ther pro-
miſes never obſerued, farther then they liſte. Therfore
tell thy maſter, firſt that he ſhall neuer be compriſed
in any league where in I am a confederate, & alſo
that I ſuſpeĉtyng his treuth (as now the dede proueth)
haue left an earle in my realme at home whiche ſhalbe
able to defende him and all his powre, for we haue
prouided ſo that he ſhall not fynde our land deſtitute
of people as he thynketh to do ; but thus ſaye to thy
maſter, that I am the very owner of Scotlãd and yᵗ he
holdeth it of me by homage,¹ and in ſo much as now
contrary to his bounden duety he beinge my vaſſall,
doth rebell againſt me, wᵗ Gods help I ſhal at my
returne expulſe him his realme and ſo tell hym : ſir
ſayd the Kyng of Armes, I am his naturall ſubieĉte &
he my naturall lord, & yᵗ he commaundeth me to ſay, I

¹ See Ballad :—
  "Now muſt ye knowe our Kynge for your regent/
  your ſouerayne lorde and preſedent/"

may boldely fay wᵗ fauor, but the commaundementes of
other I may not, nor dare not faye to my fouereigne
lord, but your letters may with your honour fent,
declare your pleafure, for I may not fay fuche woordes
of reproche to him whome I owe only my allegeaunce
& fayth.   Then fayd the Kyng, wherfore came you
hyther, will you receyue no aunfwere? yes fayde
Liõ your anfwere requireth doyng and no writynge,
that is, that immediately you fhould returne home :
Well faid the Kyng I wyll returne to your domage at
my pleafure, and not at thy mafters fomonyng.   Then
the Kyng commaunded garter to take hym to his tente
& make him good chere, which fo dyd, and cherifhed
him wel for he was fore appalled : after he was
departed the Kynge fent for all the chefe capitaynes,
and before them and all his counfaill caufed the letter
to be redde, the trewe tenor whereof foloweth woorde
by worde.

CHAPTER VII.

Continuation.

THE LETTER OF THE KYNG OF SCOTTES.[1]

IGHT excellent, right high, and mighty Prince, our deereſt brother & Couſyng, we commaunde vs vnto you in our mayſt harty maner, & receuyed fra Raff heraulde your letters quhatuntill, you approue and allow the doynges of your commiſſioners lately beyng with ours, at the borders of bathe the realmes for makyng of redreſſe, quylke is thought to you and your counſell ſhould be continuet and delaet to the xv daye of October. Als ye write ſlaars by ſee aught not cõpere perſonally, but by their attorneis. And in your other letters with our herauld Ilay ye aſcertaine

---

[1] This letter, and Henry's reply, appear alſo in Harl. MSS. 2252, and in Holinſhed, but as the variations between them are ſo very trifling, I ſtill quote Hall.

vs ye will nought entre into the treux taken between
the maſt Chriſtian kyng and your father of Aragon
becauſe ye and others of the hale liege, neither ſhould
ne make peace, treux nor abſtinēce of warre with
your common enemy without conſent of all the Confederates. And that the Emperour Kyng of Aragon,
ye and euery of you be bounden to make actual warre
this inſtant ſommer agaynſt your common enemie.
And that ſo to do is concluded and openly ſworne in
Paules kyrke at London vpon ſaincte Markes daye
laſt by paſt. And ferther haue denyed ſaue conduyte
vpon our requeſtes yᵗ a Seruitor of ours might haue
reſorted your preſence, as our herauld Ilay reportes :
Right excellēt, right high, and mightie Prince our
dereſt brother and Couſyng, the ſayd metyng of our
and your commiſſioners at the borders, was peremp-
torily appoynted betwyxt you and vs eftir diuers dietes
for reformaciõ before contynued to the Commiſſioners
metynge, to effecte that due redreſſe ſuld haue ben
made at the ſayde metynge, lyke as for our parte our
Commiſſioners offered to haue made that tyme ; and
for your part na malefactour was then arreſted to the
ſayde diet. And to gloſe the ſame, ye nowe wright,
that ſlaars by ſee nede not compere perſonally, but by
their attourneys, quylk is agayne lawe of GOD and man.
And get in crimenall accion, all ſlaars ſulde nought
compere perſonally, na punicion ſulde folowe for
ſlaughter, and than vane were it to ſeke farther

metynges or redreſſe. And hereby apperes as the
dede ſhewes that ye wyll nouther kepe gude weyes of
iuſtice and equitie nor kindnes with vs, the greate
wronges and unkyndnes done before to vs and our
lyeges we ponderate quhilk we haue ſuffered this long
time in vp beryng, maynſwering, nounredreſſyng of
Attemptates, ſo as the byll of the taken of in haldynge
of baſtard Heron with his complices in your cuntre,
quha ſlewe our wardan vnder traiſt of dayes of metynge for juſtice and thereof was filat and ordaynt to
be delyuered in ſlaynge of our liege noblemen vnder
colour by your folkes, in takynge of vthers oute of
our realme, priſonet and cheinet by the cragges in
your cõtre, withhalding of our wives legacie promiſt
in your diuerſe letters for diſpite of vs, ſlaughter of
Andrewe Barton by your awne commaund quha than
had nought offended to you nor your lieges unre-
dreſſed, and breakynge of the amitie in that behalfe
by your dede, and with haldynge of our ſhippes and
artilarie to your vſe, quharupon eft our diuerſe requi-
fitions at your wardens, Commiſſioners, Ambaſſadors,
and your ſelfe, ye wrate & als ſhewe by vthers vnto
vs, that ful redreſſe ſuld be made at the ſayde metynge
of Commiſſioners, and ſa were in hope of reformacion
or at the leſt ye for our ſake walde haue defiſted fra
inuaſion of our frendes and Couſynges with in their
awne countreis that haue nought offended at you as
we firſte required you in favoure of oure tendre Cou-

fynge the duke of Geldre, quham to deftroye and
difinherite ye fend your folkes and dudde that was in
them.   And right fa we latly defyred for our brother
and Coufynge the maft Chriften kynge of Fraunce,
quham ye haue caufed to tyne his countre of Mil-
laigne, and now inuades his felfe quha is with vs in
fecunde degree of blude, and hafe ben vnto you kynde
witoute offenfe, and more kyndar than to vs : not-
withftandynge in defenfe of his perfone we mon take
parte, and therto ye becaufe of vthers haue gyuen
occafion to vs and to our lyeges in tyme by paft,
nouther doynge iuftly nor kyndely towardes vs, pro-
cedynge alwayes to the vtter deftruction of our nereft
frendes, quha mon doo for vs quhan it fhall be neceffarie.   In euill example that yᵉ wyll hereafter be better
vnto vs quham ye lightlye fauoure, manifeftly wranged
your fifter for our fake in cõtrary our writtes.   And
fayeng vnto our herauld that we giue you fayre wordes
& thinkes the cõtrary, in dede fuch it is, we gaue you
wordes as ye dudde vs, truftynge that ye fhoulde haue
emended to vs or worth in kyndar to our frendes for
our fakes and fuld nougtight haue ftopped oure fer-
uitors paffage to laboure peax, that thei might as the
papes halines exherted vs by his brevites to do.   And
ther apon we were contented to haue ouerfene our
harmes & to haue remitted the fame, though vther
informacion was made to our haly father pape Iuly
by the Cardinall of Yorke your Ambaffadour.   And

fen ye haue now put vs fra all gude beleue through
the premiffes, and fpecially in denyenge of faueconduyte
to our feruauntes to reforte to your prefence, as your
ambaffador doctor weft inftantly defyred we fulde
fende one of our counfayll vnto you apon greate matters, and appoynctyng of differentes debatable betwyxt
you and vs, furtheryng of peax yf we might betwyxte
the moft Chriften Kyng and you, we neuer harde to
this purpofe faueconduite denied betwixte infideles.
Herefore we write to you this tyme at length playnes
of our mynde, that we require and defyre you to
defifte fra farther inuafion and vtter deftructiõ of our
brother and Coufyng the mayft Chriften Kyng, to
whome by all confederacion bloude and alye and alfo
by new bande, quhilk ye haue compelled vs lately to
take through your iniuries and harmes without remedy
done daily vnto vs, our lieges and fubdites, we are
boundē and oblift for mutuall defence ilke of vthers,
like as ye and your confederates be oblift for mutuall
inuafions and actual warre : Certifieng you we will
take parte in defence of our brother and Coufyng yᵉ
maift Chriften Kyng. And wil do what thyng we
trayeft may craft caufe you to defift fra perfuite of
him, and for denyt and pofpoynct iuftice to our lieges
we mon gyue letters of Marque accordyng to the
amitie betwixte you and vs, quharto ye haue had
lyttell regarde in tyme by paft, as we haue ordaint
our herauld the bearer hereof to faye, gife it like you

to here him and gyf him credence : right excellent right high and mighty Prince our dereſt brother and Couſyng, the Trinitie haue you in kepyng.   Geuen vnder our ſignet at Edynborowe the xxvi daie of July.

When the Kynge rede this letter, he ſente it in all haſte to the Earle of Surrey into England, whyche then lay at Pomfrett, and cauſed another letter to be deuiſed to the Kyng of Scottes, the Copie where of foloweth.

Right excellent, right high, and mighty prince &c, and haue receiued your writyng, Dated at Edenburgh the xxvi daie of July by your heraulde Lyon this bearer, wherein after reherſall and accumulaciõ of many ſurmiſed iniuries grefes and damages doone by vs & our ſubiectes to you and your lieges, the ſpecialites whereof were ſuperfluous to reherſe, remembryng that to theim and euery of theim in effect reaſonable aunſwere founded vpon lawe and cõſcience hath tofore ben made to you and youre counſail, ye not only requyre vs to defiſte from farther inuaſion and vtter deſtruction of your brother & Couſyng the French kyng, but alſo certifie vs that you will take parte in defence of the ſayd kyng, and that thyng whiche ye truſt may rather cauſe vs to defiſte, from perſuite of him, with many contriued occaſions and cõmunications by you cauſeles ſought and imagened, ſownynge to the breache of yᵉ perpetuall peace, paſſed, concluded & ſworne, betwixte you and vs, of which your im-

magened querelles caufeles deuifed to breake with vs
contrarye your othe promifed, al honor and kyndneffe:
We cannot maruayle, confideryng the auncient accuf-
tomable maners of your progenitours, whiche neuer
kept lenger faythe and promife than pleafed theym.
Howebeit, yt the loue and dread of God, nighnes of
bloud, honour of the world, lawe and reafon, had
bound you, we fuppofe ye woulde neuer haue fo farre
proceded, fpecially in our abfence. Wherein the Pope
and all princes Chriftened may well note in you, dif-
honorable demeanour whan ye lyeing in awayte feke
the waies to do that in our fayde abfence, whiche ye
woulde have ben well aduifed to attempte, we beynge
within our realme and prefent: And for theuident
approbation hereof, we nede none other proues ne
witneffe but youre owne writynges heretofore to vs
fent, we beyng within our realme, wherein ye neuer
made mencion of takynge parte with our enemie the
Frenche kynge, but paffed the tyme with vs tyll after
our departure from our faid realme. And now percafe
ye fuppofynge vs too farre from our fayde realme to
be deftitute of defenfe agaynft your inuafions, have
vttered the olde rancour of your mynde whiche in
couert maner ye haue longe kept fecrete. Neuer the
leffe, we remembrynge the brytilnes of your promyfe
and fufpectynge though not wholy beleuyng fo much
vnftedfaftnes, thought it right expedient and neceffarie to put our faide realme in a redynes for refiftyng

of your fayde enterprifes, hauyng firme truft in our
Lorde GOD and the right wytnes of our caufe with
thaffiftence of our confederates and Alies wee fhalbe
able to refyfte the malice of all Scyfmatyques and
their adherentes beyng by the generall counfayll ex-
preffely excommunicate and interdyfted, truftynge
alfo in tyme conveniente to remember our frendes, and
requyte you and our enemies, whiche by fuch vnnaturall demeanour haue given fufficiente caufe to the
dyfherifon of you and your pofteritie for ever from
the poffybilitie that ye thynke to haue to the royalme,
whiche ye nowe attempte to inuade. And yf the
example of the kyng of Nauarre beynge excluded
from his royalme for affiftence gyuen to the Frenche
kyng cannot reftrayne you frõ this vnnaturall deal-
ynge, we fuppofe ye fhall haue lyke affiftence of the
fayde Frenche kynge as the kyng of Nauarre hath
nowe: Who is a kyng withoute a realme, and fo the
Frenche kynge peaceably fuffereth hym to contynue,
wherunto good regarde woulde be taken. And lyke
as we heretofore touched in thys oure wrytyng, we
nede not make any farther aunfwere to the manyfolde
greues by you furmyfed in your letter: for as muche
as yf any lawe or reafon coulde haue remoued you
from your fenfuall opinions, ye haue ben many and
often tymes fufficientely aunfwered to the fame:
Excepte only to the pretended greues touchynge the
denyeing of our faufeconduyte to your Ambaffadoure

too bee laſt ſent vnto vs: Where vnto we make this
aunſwere, that we had graunted the ſaid ſaufe conduite,
and yf your herauld would haue taken the ſame with
hym lyke as he hath ben accuſtomed to ſollicitee
ſaufeconduytes for marchauntes and others heretofore, ye might as ſone have had that as any other, for
we neuer denyed ſaufeconduyte to any your lieges to
come vnto vs & no further to paſſe, but we ſee wel
lyke as your ſayde herauld hath heretofore mad
ſiniſter reporte contrary to trouthe ſo hath he done
nowe in this caſe as is manifeſt and open. Fynally as
towchyng your requiſition to deſiſte from farther
attemptyng againſte our enemy the French kyng, we
knowe you for no competent iudge of ſo high auctho-
ritie to requyre vs in that behalfe; wherfor God
willyng we purpoſe with the ayde and aſſiſtence of
our confederates & Alies to perſecute the ſame, and
as ye do to vs and our realme, ſo it ſhalbe remēbred
and acquited hereafter by the helpe of our lord and
our Patrone ſainct George. Who righte excellente,
right highe and myghtie Prince &c. Geuen vnder
our ſignet in our campe before Tyrwyn the xii daye
of Auguſt.[1]

When this letter was written and ſealed, the Kynge

---

[1] This date ſhows that Lyon was waiting for the King on his
return from meeting Maximilian—the anſwer muſt have been
written the next day.

Skelton evidently ſaw copies of theſe letters immediately

fent for Lyon the Scottyfh heraulde and declared to
hym that he had wel confidered his mafters letter,
and therto had made a reafonable anfwere, and gaue
to hym in rewarde a hundred angels, for which rewarde
he humbly thãked the kyng and fo taried with gartier
al night, and euer he fayde that he was fory to thynke
what domage fhoulde be done in Englande by his
Mafter or the kynge returned, and fo the nexte daye
he departed into Flaunders wyth hys Letter to haue
taken fhyppe to fayle in to Scotlande, but or he
coulde haue fhyp and wynde hys mafter was flayne."

after their arrival in England—as he makes ufe of the very
phrafeology—" Who is a Kynge withoute a realme," when fpeak-
ing of the King of Navarre.

CHAPTER VIII.

EANWHILE the Earl of Surrey, who had been left by Henry to look after the Scots, and who had promifed " fo to do my duety that your grace fhall fynde me diligent, and to fulfill your will fhalbe my gladnes," fent Sir William Bulmer to look after the Border land. And it was lucky he did fo, for " one daye in Auguft, the lorde Chamberlayne and Warden of Scotland with vii or viii 앃 men with banner difplayed entered into England and brent and haryed a great praye in Northumberland ; that hering Syr Williã bulmer called to hym the gentelmen of the borders with his archers and al they were not a thoufand men. And when they were nere affembled they brought thẽ felfes in to a brome felde called Mylfeld, where the Scottes fhould paffe. And as yᵉ Scottes proudely returned with their pray, the Englifhmen brake oute, and the

Scottes on fote like men them defended, but the arches fhotte fo holy together, that they made y᷈ᵉ Scottes geve place and v or vi hundred of them were flayne, and iii hundred or more taken prifoners, and the pray reckned befide a great nūber of geldinges that were taken in the countrey, and the lorde Hume lorde Chamberlayne fled and his banner taken."

This was an unlucky beginning for the Scots, and it had the effe&t of caufing James to take the fatal refolution of invading England. But he did not enter into it heartily, and the fuperftitious of that age after-wards called to mind feveral portents in conne&tion with the commencement of the campaign. Lindfay mentions one or two, " Att this tyme the king came to Lithgow quhair he was at the counfall verrie fad and dollorous, makand his prayeris to God, to fend him ane guid fucces in his voyage.[1] And thair cam ane man clad in ane blew gowne, belted about him with ane roll of lining, and ane pair of brottikines on his feitt, and all vther thingis conforme thairto. Bot he had nothing on his head, bot fyd hair to his fhoulderis and bald befoir. He feemed to be ane man of fiftie yeires, and cam faft forwardis, crying among the lordis, and fpeciallie for the king, faying, that he defired to fpeak with him, quhile at the laft he cam to the dafk, quhair the king was at his prayeris.

---

[1] This ftory is alfo related by Buchanan and Holinfhed.

But when he faw the king he gave him no due reverence nor falutatioun, but leined him doun gruflingis vpoun the dafk, and faid, " Sir King, my mother has fent me to the, defiring the not to goe quhair thow art purpofed, quhilk if thow doe, thou fall not fair weill in thy jorney, nor non that is with the. Fardder, fhoe forbad the, not to mell nor vfe the counfell of vomen, quhilk if thow doe, thow wilbe confoundit and brought to fhame." Be this man had fpoken thir wordis to the king, the evin fong was neir done, and the king paufed on thir wordis ; ftudieing to give him ane anfwer. Bot in the meane tyme, befoir the kingis eyis, and in the prefence of the wholl lordis that war about him for the tyme, this man evanifched away, and could be no more feine. I heard Sir David Lindfay, lyon herald,[1] and Johne Inglis the marchell, who war at that tyme young men, and fpeciall fervandis to the kingis grace, thought to have takin this man, bot they could not, that they might have fpeired farther tydingis at him, bot they could not touch him. But all thir vncouth novellis and counfall could not ftay the king from his purpofe, and vicked interpryfe, bot haifted him faft to Edinburgh to mak provifioun for himfelf and his armie againe the faid day apoyntted. That is, he had fewin great cannones out of the Caftle of Edinburgh,

---

[1] This is hardly reconcileable with the fact that Lyon was then engaged on his embaffy to Henry.

quhilkis was called the Sewin Sifteris, caftin be Robert
Borthik; and thrie mafter gunneris, furnifched with
pouder and leid to thame at thair pleafure; and in
the meane tyme they war taking out the artillarie, the
king himfelff being in the Abbey, thair was ane cry
heard at the mercatt croce of Edinburgh, about mid-
night, proclameand, as it had beine ane fummondis,
quilkis was called be the proclamer thairof, the fummondis of Platcok, defiring all earles, lordis, barrones,
gentlmen, and fundrie burgefs within the toun, to
compeir befoir his maifter within fourtie dayes, quhair
it fould happin him to be for the tyme, vnder the
paine of difobedience; and fo many as war called war
defigned be thair awin names. But whidder this
fummondis was proclaimed be vaine perfones, night
walkeris for thair paftyme, or if it was ane fpirit
I cannot tell. But on indweller in the toun, called
Mr. Richard Lawfoun, being evill difpoffed, ganging
in his gallrie, ftart fornent the croce, hearing this
voyce, thought marvell quhat it fhould be; fo he
crye[d] for his fervand to bring him his purs, and tuik
ane croun and keft it over the ftair, faying " I for my
part appealis from your fummondis and judgment, and
takis me to the mercie of God." Werrilie he quho
caufed me cronicle this was ane fufficient landit gentl-
man, who was in the toun in the meane tyme, and was
then twentie yeires of aige; and he fwore efter the
feild thair was not ane man that was called at that

tyme, that efcaped, except that on man, that appailled from thair judgmentis."

James' wife is faid to have added her entreaties to prevent the campaign, but, needlefs to fay, with no effect, and he croffed the Tweed on the 22nd Auguft, with an army [1] "whereof the brute was that they were two hundred thoufand, but for a fuertye they were an hundred thoufand good fightynge men at the left," and encamped on the banks of the Fill, a little river which flows into the Tweed. Here he feems to have remained until the 24th, during which time he iffued a proclamation, dated " Twefil hauch," (Twizell haugh), with a view to encourage his troops, ordaining " gif any man beis flane or hurt to deid in the kings army, and oift be Inglefman, or dies in the army, enduring the tyme of his oift, his aires fhall have his ward, relief and marriage, of the king fre, difpendand with his age, quhat eild that ever he be of."

The King then moved on to Norham Caftle, where, according to Holinfhed, he "ouerthrew the Barnekine, & flue diverfe within the caftle, fo that the Capteine and fuch as had charge within it, defired the King to delaie the fiege, while they might fend to the earle of Surreie alreadie come with an armie into the north parts, covenanting if they were not refcued by the nineteenth day of that moneth, they fhould deliuer

[1] Hall.

the castle vnto the King. This was granted ; and becaufe none came within the time to the refcue, the castell was deliuered at the appointed day ; a great part of it was ouerthrowne and beaten downe." Moving rapidly along the Tweed, the king took Wark Caftle, and turned inland, taking Etal and Ford.[1] Here he wafted precious time, if the old Chroniclers can be trufted, in an extremely unprofitable manner. James was always extremely fufceptible to female beauty, and, forgetful of his Wife Margaret, fuccumbed to the charms of Lady Heron of Ford,[2] if the Scotch verfion be true. Still adhering to my plan of giving contemporary hiftory if poffible, I quote the following extraƈt from Lindfay :—" Some fayes the ladie Foord being ane bewtifull voman, the King melled with hir, and the bifchope of St. Androis[3] with hir dochter, quhilk was againes the ordour of

[1] Remains of all thefe caftles ftill exift.

[2] " Sir William Heron fucceeded his brother John in the year 1498, being then 20 years old. He was high Sheriff of Northumberland in the year 1526, and died 8 July, 1535. He was twice married. By Elizabeth his firft wife, he had a fon, William, who died before him ; by the fecond, Agnes, he had no iffue."— No mention is anywhere made of a daughter of Lady Elizabeth Heron.

[3] A natural fon of James, by Margaret, daughter of Archibald Boyd of Bonfhaw, born 1495. By a difpenfation from the Pope, the King created him Archbifhop of St. Andrews, in 1509, and made him his Chancellor 1511. He was alfo the Pope's Legate a latere.

all guid captanes of warre to begin at whordome and
harlottrie, befoir ony guid fucces of battell or victorie.
But doubtles fick proceidingis is oftymes the occafioun
of ane evill fucces.   Alwayes, the King remained
thair the fpace of twentie dayes, without battell, or no
appeirance of the fame, quhill the moft pairt of thair
victuallis war fpendit, and fpeciallie the farre north-
land menis, and the illes menis, that they war forced
to goe home to furnifch the fame ; and everie lord
and barrone fend home of his fpeciall fervandis for
new provifioun ; fo that thair abod not above ten
thoufand men with the King, by bordereris and
countrie men.   Yitt the King tuik no fear, for he
beleived that the Inglifchmen fhould not have given
him battell at that tyme.   But this vicked ladye Fuird,
fieing the Kingis hoaft fo difperft, for laik of victuallis,
and knew all the fecreitis that war amongeft the
Kingis men, and the intentioun of the King himfelff,
and fecreit counfall, quhilk knawledge fhoe had be
hir frequent whordome with the King, quhilk moved
hir to afk licence of the King to pas innerward in the
countrie, to fpeak with certane of hir friendis, faying
to the King that fhoe fhould bring him all newis out
of the fouth countrie, quhat they were doeing, or
quhat was thair purpofe to doe, and thairfoir fhoe
defired the King to remane thair till hir return.   And
he againe, as an effeminat prince, fubdewed and intyfed
be this vicked voman, gave hir haiftilie credence in

this matter, and believed all that fhoe had faid to be trew. So he caufed convoy her ane litle fpace from the hoaft as fhoe defired. But this ladie Fuird being myndful to keip no credit with the King, for the loue fhoe buire to hir native countrie, fhoe paft haiftilie to the earle of Surrey, quhair he was lyand at York at that tyme, and fhew to him the haill fecreittis of the King, and how many he was, and quhair his armie lay, and quhat poyntt they war att, and how his men war difperft, and paft from him for laik of victuallis, and that thair was not abyding with him but ten thoufand of all his great armie. Quhairfoir fhoe counfalled the earle of Surrey to cum fordwadis vpoun him, affuring him of victorie, by hir ingyne, for fhoe fhould deceave the King, alfo farre as fhoe might, and put him in the Inglifmenis handis. Thir novellis being fhowin to the earle of Surrey, be this vicked voman, he greatlie rejoyced thairat, and thanked her greatumlie for hir laboures and paines, that fhoe tuik for hir native countrie promifeaud to hir, that within thrie dayes he fhould meitt the King of Scotland."

CHAPTER IX.

HETHER there is any foundation for this ſtory or not, we have it on Hall's authority that Lady Elizabeth Heron was the ſubjeᶜt of diplomatic negotiation between the Earl of Surrey and King James on 4 September in that year, the Earl then being at Alnwick. "And when all men were appoynted and knewe what too do, The erle and hys counſayll concluded and determined emonge other thynges to ſende Rouge croſſe, purſiuaunt of armes with a trompet to the kynge of Scottes with certayne in-ſtruccions, ſigned by the ſayde erle conteynynge woorde by woorde as foloweth.

Fyrſt where there hathe bene ſuyte made to the Kyng of Scottes by Elizabeth Heron, wyfe to William Heron of Forde, nowe pryſſoner in Scotlande, for caſtynge doune of the houſe or Caſtell of Forde, and as the fayde Elizabeth reporteth vppon communicacion had, the fayde kynge hath promyfed and condifcended to the fayde Elizabeth, that if fhe any tyme before none, the fift daye of September, woulde brynge and deliuer vnto hym the lorde Johnftowne, and Alexander Hume, then pryfoners that tyme in Englande, he then is contented and agreed that the fayde houfe or Caftell fhall ftande without caftynge doune, brennynge or fpoylynge the fame : Whereunto the fayde erle is content with that, vppon thys condicion, that if the fayde kynge wyll promytte the affuraunce of the fayde Caftell, in maner and forme aforefayde vnder hys feale, to deliuer the fayde lorde of Johnftowne and Alexander Hume, immediately vppon the fame affuraunce. And in cafe the fayde kynge can and will be content to delyuer the fayde Heron oute of Scotlande, then the fayde erle fhall caufe to be deliuered to the fayde kynge the two gentelmen, and two other, fyr George Hume and William Carre."

James detained Rouge Croix Purfuivant and fent his Herald Ilay on the 6th September to the Earl of Surrey, with the meffage "as touchynge the fauynge from brennynge or deftroiynge, and caftynge doune of the Caftell of Forde, for the deliueraunce of the fayde prifoners, The kyng hys mafter woulde thereto make no aunfwer."

Whilft James, however, wafted time at Ford, and his army dwindled away, Surrey was far from idle. News of James's entry into England firſt reached the Earl on the 25th Auguſt. He immediately ſummoned a general muſter at Newcaſtle on the firſt of September ; and he himſelf ſtarted for York with five hundred men, leaving the next day for Newcaſtle. At Durham he heard of the fall of Norham, and Hall goes on thus with his narrative :—" thys chaunce was more ſorowfull to the erle then to the Biſhoppe owner of the ſame. All that nyghte the wynde blewe corragiouſly, where-fore the erle doubted leaſt the lorde Hawarde hys ſonne greate Admyrall of Englande ſhoulde periſh that nyght on the ſea, who promiſed to land at Newcaſtell with a thouſand men, to accompaynie hys father, whyche promyſe he accompliſhed.

The erle harde Maſſe, and appoynted with the Prior for Sainɗte Cutberdes banner,[1] and ſo that daye beynge the thyrty daye of Auguſt he came to Newcaſtell : thither came the lorde Dacres, ſyr William Bulmer,

---

[1] Preſumably to inflame the courage of his border troops. Lambe, without mentioning his authority, gives the following de-ſcription of the banner :—" Soon after the battle of Nevil's Croſs, A. 1346, John Toſſer, prior of Durham, made a new banner, and con-ſecrated it to St. Cuthbert. The ſtaff of it was five yards long, covered with pipes, ſurmounted with a croſs, under which was a rod, as thick as a man's finger, faſtened by the middle to the ſtaff. At each end of which was a wrought knob and a little bell. All theſe except the ſtaff were of ſilver. The banner cloth of red velvet, faſtened to the rod, was a yard broad, and one yard and a quarter deep : The bottom of it was indented in five parts ; on both ſides it was embroidered, and wrought with flowers of green

fyr Marmaducke Conftable, and many other fubftanciall gentlemen, whome he reteyned wyth him as coun-fayllers, and there determined that on Sundaye next en-fuynge, he fhoulde take the felde at Bolton in Glendale, and becaufe many fouldioures were repayrynge to hym he lefte Newcaftell to the entent that they that folowed, fhoulde haue there more rome, and came to Alne-wyke the thyrde day of September, and becaufe hys fouldiars were not come, by reafon of the foule waye, he was fayne to tarye there all the fourthe daye beynge Sundaye, whyche daye came to hym the lord Admyrall hys fonne with a compaignye of valyaunt Capitaynes and able fouldiars and maryners, whiche all came from the fea, the commynge of hym muche reioyced hys father, for he was very wyfe, hardy, and of greate credence and experience."

filk and gold. In the midft of it was a fquare half yard of white velvet, whereon was a crofs of red velvet, on both fides of the cloth. In it was enclofed that holy relique, the corporax cloth, wherewith St. Cuthbert covered the Chalice, when he faid mafs. The banner cloth was fkirted with a fringe of red filk and gold ; and at the bottom of it hung three filver bells."

CHAPTER X.

BATTLE OF FLODDON FIELD.

AVING traced the courſe of Scottiſh hiſtory to this point, we may continue it by means of the account of the battle of Floddon Field, two leaves of which were bound up, as already related, in the cover of the ſame book as the "Ballade of the Scottyſhe Kynge;" and this is all the more appropriate, not only on account of the aſſociation of the piece in queſtion, but becauſe it is ſcarce, was contemporary, and was printed by the ſame printer. The tract in Mr. Chriſtie Miller's poſſeſſion is unique. It was purchaſed by the Marquefs of Blandford, and at the ſale known as White Knights' Library in 1819, was ſold for £13 13s. It has, however, been reprinted in its mutilated condition, firſt in 1809, "under reviſe of Mr. Haſlewood;" and ſecondly in 1822, at Newcaſtle, by Wm. Garrett.

❡ Hereafter enſue the trewe encountre or . .
Batayle lately don betwene . Englãde and : Scotlande.
In whiche batayle the Scottſhe Kynge was ſlayne.

❡ The maner of thaduauceſynge of my lord of
Surrey treſourier and . Marſhall of . Englande and
leuetenute generall of the north pties of the ſame
with . xxvi . M. men to wardes the kynge of . Scott/
and his . Armye vewed and nombred to an/ hundred
thouſande men at/ the leeſt.

Firſte my ſayd Lorde at his beynge at Awnewik in Northumbrelande the . iiij . daye of . Septembre the .v. yere of y⁰ Reygne of kynge Henry the .viii. herynge that y⁰ kynge of Scottes thenne was re-moued from Norhme. And dyd lye at forde . Caſtel/ & in thoſe ptyes dyd moche hurte in ſpoylyng robynge/ and brennynge/ ſent to the ſayde kynge of Scottes Ruge Cros purſeuaunte at . Armes to ſhewe vnto hym that for ſo moche as he the ſaid Kynge con-trary to his honour all good reaſon & conſcyence And his oothe of Fidelite for y⁰ ferme entartnynge of perpetuall peas betwene the kyng/ hygnes our . Souerayne lorde and hym had inuaded this Raalme/ ſpoylad brente and robbyd dyuers and ſondery townes and places in the ſame. Alſo had caſte and betten downe the Caſtel of Norhme And crewella had murdered & ſlayne many of the kynnes liege people he was comen to gyue hym bayta. And de-ſyred hym y⁰ for/ ſo moche/ as he was a kynge and a great Prynce he wolde of his luſty & noble courage coſent therunto and tarye y⁰ ſame. And for my ſayde Lordes partie his lordeſhyp promyſed ye aſſured Accomplyſshement and perfourmauce therof as he was true knyght to god and the kynge his mayſter The kynge of ſcottes herynge this/ meſſage reynued & kept w⁰ hym y⁰ ſayd Ruge Cros purſenanta & wolde nat ſuffre hym at y⁰ tyme to retourne agayne to my ſayde lorde.

The .v. daye of Septembre his lordſhyp in his ap-
prochynge nyghe to the borders of . Scotlande/ muſ-
tred at Bolton in glendayll & lodged that nyght
therein yᵗ felde with all his Armye.

❧ The nexte daye beynge the .vi daye of Septembre the kynge of ſcottes ſent to my ſayd lor of
Surrey ā harolde of his called Ilaye and demaunded
if that my ſayde Lorde wolde iuſtefye the meſſage
ſent by the ſayd purſeuaunte ruge cros as is aforeſayd
ſygneſyinge that if my lorde wolde ſo doo/ it was the
thynge/ that mooſt was to his . Ioye end comforte.
To this/ demaunde/ my lord made anſwere afore
dyuers lordes/ knyghtes and gentylme nyghe . iij myles
from the felde where ys the ſayde harolde was
apſtoynted to tarye bycauſe he ſhulde nat vewe the
Armye that he coumaunded nat oonly the/ ſayde .
Ruge cros to ſpeke and ſhewe the ſeyde werdes of
his meſſage⸗ But alſo gaue and comytted vnto hym
the ſame by . Inſtruccion ſygned/ and ſubſcrybed/
with his owne hande/ whiche my ſayde lorde ſayd/ he
wolde . Iuſtefye/ and for ſo moche as his lordſhyp
conceyued by the/ ſayde . Harolde/ how . Joyous and
comfortabe his meſſage/ was to yᵉ ſayde Kynge of
ſcottes he therfore for the more aſſuraunce of his
weſſage ſhewed that he wolde be boūden in . x.Mli. &
good ſuertes with his . Lordſhyp to gyue the ſayde
kynge batayle by Fridaye/. next after at the/ furtheſt/
If that the ſayde kynge of/ ſcottes wolde/ aſſyne and

F

appoynte any/ other Erle or Erles of his/ Realme to
be bounden in lyke maner that he wolde abyde my
fayde/ lordes commynge　And for fomoche as the
fayd kynge of . Scottes reeyuued ftyll with hym Ruge
Cros purfeuaute and wolde nat fuffre hym to retourne to my lorde my/ fayde lorde in lyke and
femblable maner dyd kepe/ with/ hym the fcottefshe
Harolde . Ilay and fant to the fayd kynge of
fcottes with his anfwere and further offer/ as is/
afdre reherfed/　A gentylman of fcotlande that accompanyed and came to my fayde lorde wich the
fayd Harolde . Ilay/　And thus . Ilay contynued
and was kepte clofe tyll the commynge home of
Ruge cros whiche was the next daye after/[1]　And
thenne/ Ilay was put at large and lyberte to retourne

---

[1] According to Hall, Rouge Croix had a narrow efcape :—
" You haue harde before, howe Ilay the Scottifshe Heraulde
was returned for Rouge Croffe, and as fone as Rouge Croffe was
returned he was difcharged, but he taryed with Yorke an Englifhe
Heraulde makynge good chere, and was not returned that mornynge
that Rouge Croffe came on hys meffage, wherefore Rouge Croffe
and hys trompet were detayned by the feruaunte of Ilay, whiche
the daye before went for Rouge Croffe, affurynge them that if
Ilay came 'not home before none, that he was not liuinge, and
then they fhoulde haue their heddes ftryken of, then Rouge Croffe
offered that hys fervaunt fhould go for Ilay, but it would not be
excepted, but as hap was Ilay came home before none, and
fhewed of his gentell enterteynynge, and then Rouge Croffe was
deliuered, and came to the Englifhe armye, and made reporte as
you haue hearde."

to the kynge of fcottes his mayftere to fhewe my
lordes anfweres declaracyons and goodly/ offers as he
had hade in euery behalue of my fayde lorde.

❧ The fame daye my Lorde deuyded his Arme
in two betaylles that is to wytte in a vauwarde and a
rerewarde and ordeyned my lorde Hawarde Admorall
his fone to be . Capitayne of the fayde vaunwarde/
and hymfelfe to by chefe Capitayne of the rerewarde.

❧ In the brefte of yᵉ fayde vauuwarde was wt
the fayde Lord Admorall ix . thoufande men and
vnder Capitaynes of the fams brefte of the batayle
was the lord . Lumley⸗ fyr Wyllm Bulmer⸗ the baron
of Hylton and dyuerfe other of the Byfshopryche of
Durefme⸗ under . Seynt⸗ Cuthbert/ banner the lorde .
Scrope of vpfall/ the lorde Ogle/ fyr wyllyam Gaf-
coygne/ fer Criftofer warde/ fyr John Gueringhm
fir walter Griffith/ fyr John Gower⸗ and dyuers othes
Efquyres and gentylmen of ẏorkefhyre and North-
umberlaed/ And in ayther wynge of the fame
batayle was iii M . men.

❧ The Capitayne of the right wynge was mayfter
Edmonde hawarde fone to mẏ feydc lorde of Surrey/
And with hym was fyr Thomas Butler/ fyr . John
Boothe fyr Richarde Boolde/ and dyuerfe other
Efquyers/ & gentylmen of Lancafshyre end Chaf-
fhyre.

❧ The Capitayne of the lafte wynge was olda fyr
Marmaduke. Cofteble & with hym was mayfter

wyllm Percy his fona . Elawe willm Conftable his broder/ fyr. Robert Conftabla mamaduke Conftable willm Conftable his fones/ And fyr John Coftable of holdernes with dyuerfe his kynnefmen Allies and othea Gentylmen of yorkefhyre and Northumberlande.

❡ In the brefte of batayle of the fayde rerewarde was . vM. mon with my falde lorde of . Surrey/ and vnder. Capitaydes of the fame was the lord Scrope of Bolton fyr Philype Tyney broder Elawe to my fayd lord of. Sur.rey George darcy fone and heyre to the lorde Darcy,[1] Sir Philipe Tylney broder in law to my faid Lorde of Surrey, Sir John Rocliff, Sir Thomas Methine, Sir William Scargill, Sir John Normavell, Sir Rauff Ellircar, Sir Ric. Abdeburghe, and dyuers oder Efquyers gentillmen and comyns of Yorkfhir. And in ather wynge of the faid rerewarde was. iij. thoufande men.

❡ The Capitaine of the right wynge, was the lord Dacre of the Northe and with hym. xv. C. of the Busfhop of Eleis men, fent frome out of Lankafhir,

---

[1] Here begins the miffing portion found in the book-cover, which is taken from a MS. in the poffeffion of the late David Laing, Efq., LL.D. V.P.S.A. Scot., read by him before the Society, March, 1867, the accuracy of which, compared with the printed text he guarantees. Dr. Laing, with refpect to the reproduction of the text, gives the following explanatory notice : " It is now printed with no other alterations, than correcting the punctuation, rejecting ordinary contractions in MSS. or printed books of that age, and ufing capital letters for proper names."

And the capitaine of the left wyng of the said rerewarde, was Sir Edwarde Stanley accompanyed hooly
with dyuers knyghtts and gentilmen of Lancaſhire.

⁌ My lorde of Surrey beyng thus ordered and
accompenyed as is aforeſaid removed upon. vi. myles
to a ffelde callid Woller Haghe withynne. iij. myles
of the king of Scottes, wher as euery man myght ſe,
how the ſaid King of Scottes did lye with his Army
vpon an high hill in the egge of Cheviotte, withynne
.ij. myles of Scotlande, wherunto he had remoued from
Forde Caſtell, ovir the watir of Till, and was enclooſed
in thre parties, with three great mountaynes, ſoe that
ther was noe paſſage nor entre vnto hym but oon
waye, wher was laied marvelous and great ordenance
of gonnes, that is to wit. v. great curtalles. ij. great
colveryns. iiij. Sacres and. vi. great Serpentynes as
goodly gounes as haue bene ſene in any realme. And
beſide theme, wher othir dyuers ſmall ordenances.
and the ſame day at night my Lorde and all the
army did lye upon the ſaid grounde callid Woller
Haghe.

⁌ And conceiving the ſaid King of Scottes to lye
ſoe ſtronglye as is aforeſaid, and that ther was a fair
plaine at the nethir parte of the ſaid mountaines callid
Mylnfelde, my ſaid Lorde of Surrey tarryed vpon the
ſame grounde. all the next daye. the. vij. day of Sep-
tembr and the nyght after truſtyng that the King
wolde haue remoued dounwade to the ſaid grounde to

have gyven hym battell. And feyng that the faid King of Scottes contynued ftill in the fame mountaine without remouyng in any wife and all his oofte with hym, my faid Lorde doutyng of the faid Kings aboid and tarrying, becaufe it was fufpect he wolde haue fled away in the night, infomyche that he was withynne. ij. myles of his oune realme fent unto hym Ruge Cros purfivannte at harmes. And eftfoones requyred hym to come doune to the faid plaine of Mylfeilde. wher was convenyent grounde for the metynge of twoe Armyes, or to a grounde bye callid Floddon or to any othir indifferent grounde for twoe batells to feght vpon.

❧ At this tyme the King waxed angry and difpleafed towarde my faid Lorde, and wold not fpek with Ruge Cros purfivaunte but had reporte of his meffage, by a gentillman which made relacion ayeine of the fame to Ruge Cros on this maner with like termes. The King my maifter wills that ye fhall fhewe to Therle of Surrey, that it befemeth hym not being an Erle, fo largely to attempte a great prince, his grace woll take & kepe his grounde and felde at his oune pleafour, and not at the affignyng of Therle of Surrey, whoom the King my maifter fuppofeth to deall with fome wichecrafte or fawcery becaufe he procureth to feight vpon oon the faid grounde. The faid Ruge Cros having this anfwer, retorned ayeine to my Lorde and fhewed his lordfhip the fame.

❬ My faid Lorde of Surrey conceivyng that the
King of Scottes did contynually reft and remaine in
the faid foretres invironde with the faid mountain and
that he wolde not in any wife remove frome the fame
to any othir indifferent grounde to abide or gyve
batell, removed his ffelde the. viij. day of Septembre
being our Ladies day the Natiuitie, and paffed ovir
the water of Till, and contynually all that day went
with the faid hoole Army in aray, in the fight of the
faid King of Scottes, at the furtheft frome hym withynne two myles, and that night loged vnder a wod
fide callid Barmor Wode directly ayeinfte the King
aforefaid, and his army Albeit there was an hill
betwene the hooftes for avoiding the daunger of goune
fhoote, and not withftanding. iiij. or. v. daies paffed
ther was litle or noe wyne, ale, nor bere, for the
people to be refrefshed with but that all the hool army
for the moofte parte wer enforced and conftreyned of
neceffite to drynke water duryng the fame tyme and
feafon without comforte or trufte of any relieff in that
behalue. My faid Lorde of Surrey, and the faid
army, the faid daunger and wantyng of drynke not
withftanding, coragiouflye avaunced forewarde to get
betwene the faid King of Scotts and his realme of
Scotlande countenanfyng to goo towarde Scotlande or
Barwike. The faid King conceiving this and as it is
confeffed fered that my faid Lorde and the Army of
Englande wolde haue gon in to Scotlande, did caufe

his tents to be taken vp and kepyng the height of the mountaine, removed with his great power and puſaunce of people out of the ſaid great forterefs towarde Scotlande. And furthwith the Scottes by thair crafty and ſubtill emaginacion did ſett on fire all ſuch thair fylthy ſtrawe and litter wher as they did ly and with the ſame made ſuch a great and a mervelous ſmoke that the maner of thair araye therby couth not be efpyed. Immediatly, my Lorde Hawarde with the vawarde, and my Lord of Surrey with the rerewarde in thair mooſte qwyke and ſpedy maner avaunced and made towarde the ſaid King of Scotts as faſte as to thaim was poſſible in aray, and what for the hilles and ſmoke long as it was or the aray of the Scotts couth be conceived, and at the laſte, they appeired in .iiij. great batells.

❡ And as ſoone as the Scottes perceived my ſaid Lordes to be withyn the daunger of thair ordenance they ſhote ſharpely thair gounes which wer verray great, and in like maner our partye recounterde them, with thair ordenance, and notwithſtanding that othir our artillary for warre couth doe no good nor advantage to our army becauſe they wer contynually goyng and advanſyng vp towarde the ſaid hilles and mountaines, yit by the help of God our gounes did ſoe breke and conſtreyn the Scottiſhe great army that ſome parte of thaim wer enforſed to come doune the ſaid hilles towarde our army. And my Lorde Hawarde conceiving

the great power of the Scottes fent to my faid (Lorde)
of Surrey his fader and required hym to advaunce his
rerewarde and to joine his right wyng with his left
wyng for the Scottes wer of that might that the
vawarde was not of power nor abull to encounter
thaim. My faid lorde of Surrey perfitely vnderftand-
ing this with all fpede and diligence, luftely, came
forwarde and joyned hym to the vawarde as afor was
required by my faid Lord Hawarde, and was glad for
neceffite to make of two battalles oon good battell to
aventure of the faid . iiij . batelles.

℃ And for fo myche as the Scottes did kepe thaim
feuerall in . iiij . batelles therfor my Lorde of Surry and
my Lorde Hawarde fodenly wer conftreyned and enforced to devide thair army in oder . iiij . batelles and
els it was thought it fhulde haue bene to thair great
daunger and jeoperdy.

℃ Soe it was that the Lorde Chamberlaine of Scotlande [1] fayde beynge Capitayne of the firfte batayle of
the Scotths fyerfly dyd fette vpon maifter Edmonde
Hawarde . Capitayne of the vttermofte parte of
the felde at the weft fyde. And betwene them was fo
cruell batayle that many of our partie . Chesfhyre men
and other dyd flee/ And the fayd mayfter Edmonde in
maner lefte alone without focoure and his ftanderde
and berer of the fame beten and hewed in peces and
hymfel . thryfe ftryken downe to the groud. Howbeit

---

[1] Here the miffing part ends.

lyke a couragyous & an hardy yonge lufty gentylman he recouered agayne and faught hande to hade with one fir Dauy home & flewe hym with his owne handes. And thus the fayde mayfter Edmonde . was in . great perell and daunger tyll that the lorde Dacre lyke a good and an hardy knyght releued and came vnto hym for his focoure.

❡ The feconde Batayle came vpon my lorde . Hawarde. The thirde batayle wherin was the kynge of . Scottes & mofte parte of the noble men of his . Reame came fyerfly vpon my fayd lord of . Surrey/ whiche two bat019lles by the help of elmyghty god were after a greht confydelyete venquyffhed ouer comen betten downe & pvt to flyght and fewe of them efcaped. with their lyues fyr. Edwarde Stanley beynge at the vttermofte parte of the fayd rerewarde one hefte[1] partie feynge the fourth batayle redy to releue the fayde kynge of fcottes batayle/ couragyoufly⸗ and lyke a lufty and an hardy knyght dyd fette vpon the fame and ouercame & put to flyght all the fcottes in the fayd batayle. And thus by the grace focour and helpe of almyghty god victory was gyven to the Reame of . England. And all the fcottyffhe ordendnce wonne & brought to Ettell and Barwyke in . Suretie.

❡ Hereafter enfueth the names of fondry noble⸗ men of the fcottes flayne at the fayde batayle & felde called Brainfton moore./

---

[1] The eaft.

Firfte yᵉ kyng of fcotoes   Mac . Cleen.

The Archelyfshop of   Iohn of Graunte

feynt . Androwes.   The Maift of . Agwis

The byfshop of . Thyles.   Lorde . Roos.

The byfshop of Ketnes.   Lord tempyll.

The Abbot ynchaffrey.   · Lorde . Borthyke.

The Abbot of Rylwenny.   Lorde . Afkyll.

Therle of . Mountroos.   Lorde . Dawiffie.

Therle of . Craforde.   Sir Alexander Scotlon

Therle of . Argyle.   Sire Iohn home.

Therle of lennox.   Therlo . Arell . Conftable.

Therle of . Lcncar.   Lorde . Lowett.

Therle of . Caftelles.   Lorde . Forboos.

Therle of Boothwell   Lorde . Coluin.

Lorde . Elwefton.   Sir . Dauy home.

Lorde . Inderby   Cuthbert home of Faf-

Lorde . Maxwell.   caftell.

Mac Keyn.

Over & aboue the feyd pfones there at flayne of
the Scottes vewd by my lorde . Dacre the/ noumbre
of . xi . or . xii . thoufande mend And of Englyfshme
flayne and taken pryfoncrs vpon꞊ xii.C. dyuers pryfoners are taken of yᵉ fcottes But nꝙo Notable perfon
faue oonly fyr/ wyllm̄ Scotte knyght Councellour of
the fayde kynge of fcottes and as is fayd a gentylma
well lerned Alfo S͞r John Forma knyght broder to
the Byfshop of Murrey which byfshop as is reported
was &/ is mooft pryncyall procurour of this warre/

And one other called ſ̃ John Colehome many other
ſcottyſshe pryſoner . coude & myght haue been taken/
but they were ſoo vengeable & cruell in theyr fygh-
tngy that/ whenne Englyſshmen had the better of
them they wolde nat ſaue them/ though it ſo were
that dyuerſe ſcottes offered great ſumes of money for
theyr lyues.

❡ It is to be noted that the felde beganne betwene . iiij and . v. at after Noone and contynued
within nyght if it had fortuned to haue ben further
afore nyght many mo ſcottes had ben ſlayne and taken
pryſoners louynge beto almyghty god all the noble
men of Englande tha were vpon the ſame felde bothe
lordes and Knyghtes are ſafe from any hurte/ And
none of theym awantynge ſaue oonly maiſter Harrgy
Gray ſyr Huinfeide lyle bothe pryſoners in Scotlade
ſyr John . Gower of yorkeſhyre and ſyr John Boothe
of Lancaſshyre both wantynge and as yet nat founden.

❡ In this batayle the ſcottes hadde many great
Auauntagies/ that is to wytte the hyghe . Hylles and
mountaynes a great wynde with them and ſodayne
rayne all contrary to oug bowes and Archers.

❡ It is nat to be doutbted but the ſcottes fought
manly and were determyned outher to wynne yᵉ
Feld or to dye　They were alſo as well apoynted
as was poſſyble at all poyntes with Armoure & harneys ſo that fewe of them were ſlayne with arrowes
Howbeit the bylles did bete and hewe them downe
woth ſome payne and daunger to Englyſshemen.

The fayd fcottes were fo playnely determyned to abyde batayle and nat to flee that they put from them theyr horfes and alfo put of theyr botes and fhoes and faught in the vampis/[1] of theyr hoofes every man for the mooft ptie/ with a kene and a fhape fpere of . v. yerdes longe and a target aforh hym And when theyr fperes fayled and wera fpent/ then they faught with great end fharpe fwerdes makyng/ lytell or no noys/ vithoue that; that for the ptie many of them wolde defyre to be faued.

ℂ The felde where yᵉ fcottes dyd/ lodge was nat to be reprouyd but rather. to be romended greatly for there many and great nombre of goodiyl tenttes and moche good ftuffe in the fame & in the fayd felde was plentie of wyne bere ale beif multon falfyfshe chefe and other vytalles neceffary and conuenyent for fuche a great Army Albeit our Army doutynge that the fayd vytalles hadde ben poyfoned for theyr dif- truccion wolde not faue but vtterly diftroyed theym.

ℂ Hereafter enfueth the names of fuch noble men as after the Felde were made knyght/ for theyr valyance Act/ in the famc by my fayd lorde therle of Surrey.

ℂ Firfte my lorde Scrope Sir Edmonde Hawarde
 of wpfall Sir . Guy . Oawney
Sir willm Percy Sir . Raffe falwayne

---

[1] See ballad " Of the out yles ye rough foted fcottes."

Sir . Richarde. Malleuerey
Sir george Darcy
Sir . w. gafcoygne yᵉ yoger
Sir . willm. Medlton
Sir willm . Maleuerdy
Sir Thomas . Bartley
Sir marmaduke . Coftable
Sir xpofer . Dacre (yᵉ yoger
Sir . Hohn . Hoothome.
Sir. Nicholas. Appleyarde.
Sire Edwarde . Goorge
Sir . Rauf . Ellercar yᵉ
    yoges
Sir . John wyliyby
Sir. Edwarde . Echinghme
Sir . Edwarde . Mufgraue
Sir . John ftanley
Sir . walter ftonner
Sir . Nyniane martynfelde.
Sir Raffe . Bowes

Sir/ Briane ftapleton of
    wyghall.
Sir . willm . Conftable of
    Hatefelde
Sir . willm . Conftable of
    Larethorpe
Sir Xpofer . Oanby
Sir . Thomas Burght
Sir . willm . Rous
Sir . Thomas . Newton
Sir . Roger of Fenwyke
Sir . Roger Gray
Sir . Thomas Connyers
My lorde Ogle
Sir . Thomas ftrngewafe
Sir . Henri . Thwaittes
My lorde lumley
Sir . Xpofe . Pekerynge.
Sir . John Bulmer

❡ Emprynted by me. Richarde . Faques dwllyng In
    poulys churche yerde."

In this interefting and graphic defcription of the
battle of Branxton Moor, or Floddon Field, it is
worthy of notice that there is no account of the death
of King James. It fimply records the fact that the
King and his fon were flain; and, as no mention is

made of his body being found, it is probable the
poem was written on the ſpot before the diſcovery.

All accounts agree as to the perſonal bravery of
the King; although the ſuperſtition of the times, as
noted by Holinſhed, told upon him. " There
chanced alſo manie things taken (as yee would ſay)
for warnings of ſome great miſchance to follow,
which though ſome reputed but as vaine and caſuall
haps; yet the impreſſion of them bred a certeine
religious feare and new terror in his heart. For as
he was in councell with his lords, to vnderſtand their
opinions touching the order of his battels, there was
an hare ſtart amongſt them, which haueing a thouſand
arrowes, daggers, and other kind of things beſtowed
at hir, with great noiſe and ſhowting, yet ſhe eſcaped
from them all ſafe and without hurt. The ſame
night alſo, miſe had gnawne in ſunder the buckle and
leather of his helmet wherewith he ſhould faſten the
ſame to his hed. And moreouer, the cloth or veile
of his inner tent (as is ſaid) about the breake of the
day, appeared as though the deawic moiſture thereof
hed beene of a bloudie colour."

King James, fancying that the Engliſh were giving
way, diſmounted from his horſe, and, in ſpite of re-
monſtrances from his friends, charged the enemy,
who were, however, reinforced by Edward Stanley
and his diviſion, and the Scots were thoroughly

routed; the King, and all with him, being flain. Hall
fpeaks moft highly of the King's prowefs in the following panegyric : " O what a noble and triumphant
courage was thys for a kyng to fyghte in a battayll
as a meane fouldier : But what auayled hys ftronge
harnes; the puyffaunce of hys myghtye champions
wyth whome he defcended the hyll, in whome he foo
much trufted that with hys ftronge people and great
number of men, he was able as he thought to haue
vanquifhed that day the greateft prynce of the world,
if he had ben there as the erle of Surrey was, or elfe
he thought to do fuch an hygh enterprice hym felfe
in hys perfon, that fhould furmount the enterprifes of
all other princes : but how foeuer it happened God
gaue the ftroke and he was no more regarded then a
poore fouldier, for all went one way.   So that of his
awne bataill none efcaped but fyr William Scot
knight his chauncelour, and fyr Jhon forman knight,
his feriaunt Porter, whiche were taken prifoners, and
w^t great difficultie faued."

The body of the King having been ftripped by
marauders, was not found until the following
day :—

" Well knowen it was by them that fought, and alfo
reported by the pryfoners of Scotlande, that theyr
kynge was taken or flayne, but hys body was not
founde tyll the next daye, becaufe all the meane
people as well Scottes as Englyfhe were ftrypped oute

of theyr apparell as they laye on the felde, yet at the
lafte he was founde by the Lord Dacres, who knew
hym well by hys pryuye tookens in that fame place
where the battayle of the Earle of Surrey and hys,
firfte ioyned together.

Thys kynge had dyuerfe deadely woundes and
in efpeciall one with an Arowe, and an another wyth
a byll as apered when he was naked. After that the
bodye of the kynge of Scottes was found and
brought to Barwycke, the Earle fhowed yt too Syr
Wyllyam Scott hys Chaunceller and Syr Jhon
Forman hys feriante porter, whiche knewe hym at
the fyrfte fighte and made greate lamentacyon. Then
was the bodye bowelled, embawmed, and cered, and
fecretly amongeft other ftuffe conueyed to Newcaftell.
* * * * * After thys noble vyctorye therle wrote
fyrfte to the Quene whiche had rayfed a greate power
to refifte the fayde Kynge of Scottes, of the wynnynge
of the battayle, for then the bodye of the kynge of
Scottes was not fownde, and fhe yet beynge at the
towne of Buckyngham had woorde the next daye
after that the kynge of Scottes was flaine, and a parte
of hys coate armure to her fente,[1] for whiche victorye
fhe thanked GOD, and fo the Earle after that the
Northe parte was fett in a quietnes, returned to the

---

[1] His gauntlet. His fword and dagger are among the moft
precious relics preferved in the Heralds' College.

G

Queene with the deade body of the Scottyfshe Kyng
and broughte it to Richemond."

From Richmond the royal remains were taken to
the adjoining monaftery of Sheen, in accordance with
the teftimony of Stowe, who fays :—" After the
battle, the bodie of the fame King being found, was
clofed in lead, and conveyed from thence to London,
and to the monafterie of Sheyne in Surry, where it
remained for a time, in what order I am not certaine ;
but fince the diffolution of that houfe, in the reygne
of Edward the Sixt, Henry Gray, Duke of Suffolke,
being lodged, and keeping houfe there, I have been
fhewed the fame bodie fo lapped in lead, clofe to the
head and bodie, throwne into a wafte room amongft
the old timber, lead, and other rubble. Since the
which time, workmen there, for their foolifh pleafure,
hewed off his head ; and Lancelot Young, mafter
glazier to Queen Elizabeth, feelinge a fweet favour
to come from thence, and feeing this fame dried from
all moifture, and yet the form remaining, with the
haire of the head and beard red, brought it to
London, to his houfe in Wood Street, where, for a
time, he kept it for its fweetnefs, but in the end
caufed the fexton of that church (St. Michael's,
Wood Street) to bury it amongft other bones taken
out of their charnell."

Many of the Scots refufed to believe their King to
be dead. Lindfay, referring to the Englifh fearching

for the King's body after the battle, writes thus :—
" Bot they could not find him, albeit they fond
fondry in his luferay ; for the fame day of the feild
he caufed ten to be in his awin luferay lyk vnto his
awin prefent apperell, amonges quhom was tuo of his
awin guard : the on called Alexander M'Cullo, and
the vther the fquyer of Cleifch, who war both verrie
lyk in makdome to the King ; and fo they tuik on of
thame, whom they thought lykeft to the Kyng, and
keft him in ane chariott, and had him with thame
into England ; but trew it is they gott not the King,
becaus they had nevir the tokin of his yron belt to
fchow to no Scottis man."

And in another place the fame writer declares :—
" But ten yeires thairefter ane certane man being
convict of his lyff for flauchter, offered to the duik of
Albanie to latt him fie the place quhair the King was
buried, and for the greater evidence, his yron belt befyd
him in the grave. Bot this man gott no audience
be thame that was about him, and the duik of Albanie
defired not that fick things fhould be knawin."

Such was the fad fate of " the fcottyfshe kynge "
whofe character Holinfhed fums up in the following
terms :—" This James the fourth was of a firme
bodie, of iuft ftature, of moft comelie countenance,
and of fharpe witte, but altogether vnlearned, as the
fault of that age was. But he did diligentlie applie
himfelfe to an old cuftome of the countrie, cunninglie

to cure wounds, the knowledge whereof in times paſt was a thing common to all the nobilitie, being alwaies vſed in the warres. He was eaſilie to be ſpoken vnto, gentle in his anſwers, iuſt in his iudgements, and ſo moderat in puniſhments, that all men might eaſilie ſee he was vnwillinglie drawen vnto them. Againſt the detraction of the euill, and admoniſhment of the good, there was ſuch worthineſſe of mind in him (confirmed by the quiet of a good conſcience, and the hope of his innocencie) that he would not onelie not be angrie, but not ſo much as vſe a ſharpe word vnto them. Amongeſt which vertues, there were certeine vices crept in by the ouermuch deſire to pleaſe the people, for whileſt he laboured to auoid the note of covetouſneſſe (obiected to his father) and ſought to win the favour of the common ſort (with ſumptuous feaſts, gorgeous ſhewes, and large gifts) he fell into that pouertie, that it ſeemed (if he had liued long) that he would have loſt the favour of his people (wonne in old times) by the impoſition of new taxes. Wherefore his death was thought to haue timelie happened vnto him."

To the above accounts of James and the Battle of Floddon, few notes need be added. Two or three, however, may render the ſenſe of the ballad clearer in ſome places.

" A kynge a ſomner it is wonder."—Skelton, in his

difguft at James's letter to Henry, could not fpeak ftrongly enough, fo he ufed an epithet to him which, as an ecclefiaftic, was perhaps the moft fpiteful he could employ. A fomner, or apparitor, was accounted an exceedingly mean office. Chaucer, in "the Frere's prologue," fays :—

> " A fompnour is a renner vp and doun
> With mandements afor fornicatioun
> And is ybete at euery tounes ende."

And in "the Freres tale" he enlarges, in a ftill more unfavoury manner on the office of Somner.

"thre fkippes of a pye," or three hops of a magpie, is a term ufed to denote the fmall value of James's expoftulations—fee alfo "your counfeyle was not worth a flye."

"Ye had bet better to haue bufked to huntey bakes."—Huntly bank was the place where Thomas of Erceldoune met the Fairy Queen, and is on one of the Eldoun Hills—but Skelton feems to have ufed it at random, and only for the fake of the rhyme ; thus in his verfes againft Dundas, "Dundas dronken and drowfy, fkabed, fcuruy, and lowfy," he fays :—

> "Dundas
> That dronke affe,
> That rates and rantis,
> That prates and prankes
> On Huntley bankes."

Again, in " Why come ye not to Courte " :

> " They play their olde pranckes,
> After Huntley bankes : "

and in " Howe the douty Duke of Albany," &c.,

> " And for to wright
> In the difpyght
> Of the Scottes ranke
> Of Huntley banke."

" That noble erle the whyte Lyon," was Thomas Howard, Earl of Surrey, fon of the firft Duke of Norfolk, flain at Bofworth. He himfelf was there taken prifoner, attainted, and loft the earldom—as his father had loft his dukedom—from the fact of his rebellion. After three years' imprifonment in the Tower his earldom was reftored, as was alfo his dukedom after Floddon, when an augmentation of arms was granted to him, bearing on the bend of his own arms a demi-lion of Scotland, pierced through the mouth with an arrow.

His fon, " the lorde admirall," was at the fame time created Earl of Surrey.

The white lion was the badge of the houfe of Howard, and Holinfhed explains this in the following way :—" Upon the honor of this victorie, Thomas Haward earle of Surrie (as a note of the Conqueft) gaue to his feruants this cognifance (to weare on their

left arme) which was a white lion (the beaſt which he
before beare as the proper enſigne of that houſe)
ſtanding over a red lion (the peculiar note of the
kingdome of Scotland) and tearing the ſame red lion
with his pawes."

A BALLADE OF THE SCOTTYSSHE KYNGE.

A ballade of the scottysshe kynge.

Kynge Iamy/Iomp pour. Iope is all go
He commnoed our kynge why dyde he so
To you nothyng it dyde accorde
To common our kynge pour soverayne lorde.

A kynge a somner it is wonder
Knowe ye not salte and suger asonder
In your somnynge ye were to malaperte
And your harolde no thynge experte
ye thought ye dyde it full valyauntolye
But not worth thre skyppes of a pye/.
Syr squyer galyarde ye were to swyfte.
your wyll renne before your wytte.
To be so scornefull to your alye/
your counseyle was not worth a flye.
Before the frensshe kynge/danes/and other
ye ought to honour your lorde and brother
Trowe ye syr James his noble grace/
For you and your scottes wolde tourne his face
Now ye prode scottes of gelaway.
For your kynge may synge welaway
Now must ye knowe our kynge for your regent/
your soverayne lorde and presedent/
In hym is figured melchisedeche/
And ye be desolate as armeleche
He is our noble champyon.
A kynge anoynted and ye be non
Thrugh your counseyle your fader was slayne
wherfore I fere ye wyll suffre payne/
And ye proude scottes of dunbar
Parde ye be his homager.
And suters to his parlyment/
ye dyde not your dewty therin.
wherfore ye may it now repent
ye bere your selfe som what to bolde/
Therfore ye haue lost your copholde.

ye be bounde tenauntes to his eſtate.
Gyue vp yovr game ye playe chekmate.
For to the caſtell of noꝛham
I vnderſtonde to ſoone ye cam,
For a pryſoner there now ye be
Eyther to the deuyll oꝛ the trinite.
Thanked be ſaynte.Goꝛge our ladyes knythe
your pꝛyd is paſte adwe good nytht.
ye haue determyned to make a fraye
Our kynge than beynge out of the waye
But by the power and myght of god
ye were beten weth your owne rod
By your wanton wyll ſyr at a woꝛde
ye haue loſte ſpoꝛes/cote armure/and ſwoꝛde
ye had bet better to haue buſked to huntey bakes/
Than in Englonde to playe ony ſuche pꝛankes
But ye had ſome wyle ſede to ſowe.
Therfoꝛe ye be layde now full lowe/
your power coude no lenger attayne
warre with our kynge to meyntayne.
Of the kynge of nauerne ye may take hede/
How vnfoꝛtunately he doth now ſpede/
In double welles now he dooth dꝛeme.
That is a kynge witou a realme
At hym erample ye wolde none take.
Experyence hath bꝛought you in the ſame bꝛake
Of the out yles ye rough ſoted ſcottes/
we haue well eaſed you of the bottes
ye rowe ranke ſcottes and dꝛoken danes
Of our englyſſhe bowes ye haue ſette pour banes.
It is not ſyttynge in tour noꝛ towne/

A comner to were a kynges crowne
That neble erle the whyte Lyon.
your pompe and pryde hath layдea downe
His sone the lorde admyrall is full good.
His swerde hath bathed in the scottes blode
God saue kynge. Henry and his lordes all
And sende the frenсhe kynge suche an other fall/

C Amen/ for saynt charyte=
And god saue noble.
Kynge/ Henry/
The. viij.